ONCE UPON A

DHARAMYUDH

ONCE UPON A DHARAMYUDH

Vibhor Tikiya

Srishti
PUBLISHERS & DISTRIBUTORS

Srishti Publishers & Distributors
N-16, C. R. Park
New Delhi 110 019
editorial@srishtipublishers.com

First published by
Srishti Publishers & Distributors in 2015

10 9 8 7 6 5 4 3 2 1

All characters in this book are fictitious, and any resemblance to real persons, living or dead, is coincidental.

Printed and bound in India

Dedicated to my father, Omprakash Tikiya,
who is the best institution I have ever attended,
This book is for you, Paa, and of course for Dharam.

Karmanye Vadhikaraste, Ma phaleshou kada chana,
Ma Karma Phala Hetur Bhurmatey Sangostvakarmani.

(You have the right to perform your actions, but you are not entitled to the fruits of the actions.
Do not let the fruit be the purpose of your actions, and therefore you won't be attached doing your duty.)

Dharam

Change is the law of the universe.

Life can get quite befuddling at times. At one point, you want something so bad, that you are ready to do anything about it. Life and circumstances change fast and you forget what you were ready to give everything up for.

I remember the day I laid the first stone of this institution. It represented everything – our hopes, our dreams and our duties. It had become a religion of sorts and was aptly named 'DHARAM'.

But when you try to create something good, you first have to overcome all and everything against you, including your own ethos. As I tried to create my way to realize my dreams, I came face to face with everything that made my dream seem impossible to achieve.

My battle was apparently with a man, Uday Shankar Chaubey, who had been through hell and had come out of it. He was unyielding, upright and strongly believed me to be the enemy. My true battle, however, was with a system which selectively went against firms such as ours and put us in a situation where we are forced to be servile to middlemen and touts.

Labour courts, local politicos and other establishments created to 'defend' the interests of labourers seldom do so. They made me go from pillar to post trying to find a solution to the conundrum that was Uday. Each time, I emerged poorer and weaker than before.

Dharam is the story of an institution in turmoil, a battle between the perceived haves and have-nots.

For me, it represents a more personal journey, where I gained and lost a lot. It is an expression of my love towards the people that mattered to me. Above all, it is an institution whose trial was executed in the most unconventional way possible – by fire.

The Legacy

The individual self is the traveller in the chariot of the material body and the intelligence is the driver. Mind is the driving instrument and the senses are the horses.

—Bhagvad Gita

Dharam was born out of hope and passion. Two brothers set out on a humble journey to make it big in the world of business.

Back in the 1960s, Manohar and Chand had ventured out to start something in the fabric industry. The setting was Punjab which, in the early 1960s, was relatively underdeveloped. There were hardly any industries in the state and very few people ventured into anything else except agriculture. It was a paradise with paddy plantations forming part of an agricultural largesse that defined the state.

In those days, manufacturing was considered as a risky business to enter into, so Manohar and Chand decided to get into textile trading first. They had a neat arrangement: Manohar would take care of the purchases and stock management; Chand would take care of the Sales, taking the stock on a cycle and selling it door to door.

The two brothers were quite dissimilar in their personas. Manohar was plump, dark-skinned and had a huge moustache. Chand was slim, quite fair and was clean shaven. They were also quite dissimilar in their demeanour. Manohar was the silent, conservative type while Chand was a flagrant, risk-loving individual. Both dressed quite similarly. They would wear plain shirts, vests over them and matching trousers. Except for their garb, it was difficult to believe that they were brothers. But, they made a good team since their skills complemented each other in many ways.

They had a small shop with an attached godown where they kept the fabric. One of them would always be there at the shop. It was situated in the heart of Ludhiana and was quite well-constructed. It was fully tiled which wasn't common in those days. The walls were replete with photos of the Hindu gods and that of their late father – Dharam.

Chand and Manohar sat looking at the books together. One was feeling very hopeful about the future and the other one was only filled with concern.

"One day, this business will become huge," Chand said, patting Manohar on the back.

Manohar looked at him and sighed. "The only things that are huge right now, Chand, are our bills. We have all kinds of bills. Electricity bills, material bills and oh wait, this one's the best. This is some bill from the municipal corporation for cleaning the sewage next to the company building. Wow, this is a shit bill."

"We will pay them all. You know, pay the shit bill first. If that is blocked, you will stink this place up."

"You're particularly high today, Chand."

"Yes I am, but I don't know why. Mark my words, Manohar. This firm will be huge one day and you and I will sit on the owner's chairs and manage it by just commanding people around."

But as much as they aspired for a big business, their beginning was very humble. The business wasn't easy either. They basically bought fabric from manufacturers and sold it to sub-dealers and retailers. One needed to have a good working knowledge of what the market wanted. It was all about intelligent purchases and efficient marketing. Though the business model was simple, it required a lot of ground work. There were monetary problems since it was difficult to sell and when one did manage to sell, it was on credit. Purchases were cash because manufacturers wanted their money quickly but payments were on credit and they were not very secure. Recovery of money was a problem and it often entailed Chand getting beaten up.

Chand once sold some stock to a Marwari businessman, Prashant and then went to collect his payment from him when it was due. Prashant was a tricky man to deal with.

Chand went to him in his office and said, "Sir, I had sold you some fabric two months ago. The payment for the same is due. Could you give me the money you owe me?"

Prashant looked at him with disgust, quite like the way a senior power-driven boss looks at an employee who has rubbed him the wrong way. "How dare you ask for money from me? I will give it when I want to."

"But sir, I need the money, otherwise how will I buy new stock?"

"That's not my concern."

"Sir, I'm not leaving until I get my money."

Prashant got irritated and slapped Chand on the face.

"You want your money? Here is your money. Now get lost and don't show your face around here again lest I will get you beaten up."

Chand appeared a bit shaken up but did not move an inch. "Sir, with all due respect, I am not moving until I get what you owe me."

Prashant then called some of his servants and asked them to beat Chand up. The servants ganged up on him, they kicked and punched him multiple times. He tried to hit back but was overpowered. He was bleeding when Prashant told his servants to stop. Chand lay listless on the floor for some time. After a few moments, he managed the strength to get up. Prashant then held him by the hair and said, "Do you want your money now?"

Chand replied, "You can't break me, sir. Kill me if you want to. I won't leave without my money as long as I have some life left in me."

Prashant was surprised by his reply. He had never seen such resilience. He then turned and asked one of his servants to get the money from the locker. The servant got the money and Prashant gave it to Chand.

Chand took the money, smiled and said, "Sir, would you like to see some new samples? I have got some really interesting designs."

Prashant stared at him for a moment and sighed. "You are a crazy man. Okay, show me what you've got."

Manohar was meticulous about the purchase and Chand about the sales. They were honest, fair, hardworking and conservative in spending. Together, they clicked and the business grew rapidly. They slowly expanded from one store to two and from two to four in a couple of years.

One day, when they were sitting in their office, Chand confessed to Manohar that he wasn't happy. Manohar was surprised and asked him, "Why aren't you happy? We have grown to four stores in a couple of years. We have enough money for our families. We are secure and set in our ways. We can relax now."

"We need to expand beyond this, you know. There was this man who I was talking to the other day. He gave me two suggestions. He said that we already have a market so we should invest in machines and that we should move to Bombay since the major textile market is located there."

"No, Chand. That's very risky and we don't have enough hands."

"We have the hands. You manage purchase, right? Instead of purchase, you will manage manufacturing. We can do this, you know."

"I am not sure about this, Chand. Aren't you satisfied with what we're earning right now? What about the investment?"

"We'll sell these stores and then gradually sell this stock. That way we'll have the initial investment needed for the company."

Manohar heard him out but he was still sceptical about the major transition that Chand was proposing. By nature Manohar was the one to take fewer risks and was content with what he had. Chand was the one who took the lead when it came to new projects.

"Come on! You live life only once. I don't want to die with regret knowing we did not make an attempt to grow big," continued Chand, in an attempt to convince Manohar.

"I don't know, Chand. There's also a chance that in trying to make something huge, both of us end up on the streets."

"There is a risk, Manohar. I accept that, but let us give it one chance. You live once so why think twice. One life after all."

Chand was a salesman and a good one at that. He knew that ordinarily Manohar would not have taken the move to Bombay. He was aware that Manohar was happy where he was, content with what life and God had given him. Yet, he continued trying to convince Manohar till he relented.

They decided to make the move to Bombay to pursue larger goals. Bombay, at that time, was the city of dreams. Anyone who had a vision made his or her way into this city. It was the city where dreams either came true or they burnt to ashes, leaving the dreamer devoid of much hope.

If you wanted to be in politics, you went to Delhi; if you wanted to be in the arts – Calcutta. However, Bombay was the place you went to if you wanted to grow in almost any business. It was the time when manufacturing and trading were both prevalent in this island city. It had become the financial capital of India while the other metros did not have any scope of industrial activity.

Chand decided he was going to go first, get things in place and then ask Manohar to come to Bombay. He knew Manohar would get discouraged if conditions were not right in Bombay and the plan would be over even before it began. So, he told Manohar he would call him later. It took him two-and-a-half days to reach Bombay by train. He reached the legendary Victoria Terminus station. He had never seen so many people together in one place before. There was commotion all around him and yet people seemed to know exactly where they were going.

There was commotion outside the station as well. Street-vendors, auto rickshaws and cars were all around and the whole place was buzzing with activity. It was quite overwhelming. Suddenly, he seemed so insignificant in the world order.

A man named Janardan Agarwal had made the necessary arrangements for Chand. He was to stay in a place called Mahalakshmi not far away from the station. In those days, the wholesale market for fabric was located in Kalbadevi and most of the mills were located in a place called Parel.

The next day, Chand decided to venture out to see the other mills and how they were set up. He was also slated to look at a few plots so that he could determine where he was going to set up his manufacturing and sales unit.

Chand spent a whole week shortlisting and planning his setup. He wanted a constructed facility since he did not want to waste time. At the end of the first week, he had finalized the location and had given the down payment.

The plot was located near Lower Parel. It was about a thousand square metres and there was a decently constructed shed over it which could accommodate about 120 machines. It was an industrial zone and there were other chemical and manufacturing companies in the same zone.

He talked to a lawyer and got the process of registration done. The company was registered on 31 October 1967 as M & C Limited. Manohar and Chand were the shareholders and the registered office was at Parel, the facility that Chand had purchased. Chand got the memorandum and articles of the company registered and the firm M & C came into existence.

Chand called Manohar. "Manohar, the company has been registered. We are good to go."

"Very good. What have you named the company?"

"M & C Limited after the two of us."

There was silence at the other end of the call for some time. Manohar then spoke, "May I make a suggestion about the name."

"Yeah."

"Can we name it after the one man who has mattered the most to both of us?"

"Father?"

"Yes."

"Okay."

For a moment, on both ends of the phone, the brothers quietly shed tears for their late father. They had lost him to cancer and seen him in immense pain in the last few days of his life. Chand kept the phone down. The very next day, there was an alteration made to the Memorandum of Association. The company M & C Limited was renamed to Dharam Synthetics Limited.

After that, everyone dove into action. There was not a moment to be lost since each moment wasted meant money washed down the drain.

Chand ordered the machines. He visited the facility daily and meticulously planned where he would place the machines.

Meanwhile, Manohar was winding up back in Punjab. He closed the firm, sold most of the stock and also sold the office there.

He gave Chand a call. "So you have good news. Are we all set to build our empire?"

"No. We'll be set when you come here."

"Okay. I'll book my ticket today. Are you doing alright?"

"I'm fine, but you must come quickly. We are losing potential business each day that you are not here."

Manohar moved whatever stock was left to his house and booked a ticket to Bombay. He was sceptical, slightly scared but decided that he was going to take the risk. After all these years of hearing Chand blabber about the 'One Life' philosophy, he had started believing it too.

While Chand had been overwhelmed to see the commotion in VT, Manohar was in a state of shock. He had heard stories about the big city but had never imagined the city to be this vibrant. Reality was much more startling that those stories.

He was scared to see so many people moving around in such a hurry. It was very different from the life that he had seen in Punjab where things proceeded at a relaxed pace. People hardly moved a muscle. They opened their store in the morning, would casually close it by afternoon and go home for lunch, and then would come back in the evening and work till eight. It was so comfortable, so convenient. He was already regretting his decision to come to Bombay and wondered why he had listened to Chand in the first place.

The thing that scared Manohar the most was that while they had been considered big shots in Punjab, they were nobody in Bombay.

Soon it became clear that even the money they had saved was enough for just one shot at the business. Bombay was much more expensive than they had anticipated. Once the capital was exhausted for machines, there was precious little left for raw material. They needed the first lot of fabric manufactured from the machines to come out well.

The machines came in a month's time after Manohar's arrival. Meanwhile, Manohar arranged for people who knew about textile manufacturing. He had a working knowledge of what designs worked in the industry. He just needed to understand the process of weaving and a technician to assist him.

That was when he was lucky enough to meet a man named Shah.

"How long have you worked in the industry?"

"Ten years. Sir if I may ask, which machines are you setting up?"

"Four by ones."

"I have worked on these machines, sir. I can handle them."

"Where do you stay?"

"Half an hour from the factory, sir."

"Hmm... You have to work very hard. You know we work late nights. You have to be with us."

"Okay sir. I am not afraid of hard work."

"Hmm... We will offer a hundred rupees per month."

"Okay. Done, sir."

"Can you also arrange for the labourers? Do you have any contacts?"

"Yes sir. I can. Consider that done."

"Okay then. Consider yourself hired."

Shah was a great addition to the team. After the machines arrived, he was critical about the assembling process. He knew the machines inside out and was good at what he did. Since he was so adept at handling them, there were hardly any quality defects in the fabric manufactured. Manohar kept track of the manufacturing and Chand took care of the sales. It was a dream team destined to be together.

As the entire team worked day and night, Dharam grew rapidly. The ethics, resilience and hardwork of the owners paid off and before they knew it, Dharam had a total of 100 machines and a production capacity of one lakh metres a month.

As things started settling down at the business front, Chand brought his family back to Bombay while Manohar's stayed back in Punjab.

Both Chand and Manohar had been blessed with happy and peaceful personal lives. Chand was married to Sheila and had a daughter, Anahita who had been married some years back.

Manohar was married to Vidya. He was the proud father of an academic genius, Prakash and a daughter, Nima. Prakash was a civil engineer from the Regional Engineering College, Kurukshetra. He was a simple boy, slim with an innocent but stern looking face. He had a dusky complexion and a decently large moustache which was in sync with the times then. He was a huge Rajesh Khanna fan and emulated him in whatever he wore.

Prakash was sincere to the core. He had worked hard in school, harder in college. He excelled in college and was placed in Engineers

India Limited which was a prestigious institution to work in. He was unmarried as he had not found the right girl yet.

Nima was a delicate, soft-spoken girl who had completed her graduation and was fast becoming of marriageable age.

Both the families enjoyed a good life till 1980, when things took a turn for the worse. Manohar fell sick and his condition worsened with time. He stopped going to work and the doctors gave up on him. He was in and out of the hospital many times. By January 1981, Manohar's condition was so bad that he could not even get out of his bed.

He was admitted to a hospital and the doctors tried everything that they could to bring him back to health.

The hospital was quite small. In those days, there weren't many huge hospitals and the few that did exist were only meant for the high and mighty. This one had a total of twenty hospital beds, a ventilator by each bed and basic amenities.

The relatives started paying visits to the hospital. One morning was particularly bleak and it seemed that Manohar had only a few breaths left in him. He called for Prakash.

There was a waiting room outside where people were waiting. There was enough lighting in the waiting room and a couple of fans. One could hear the sound of the fans amidst the silence. The people outside were all tense and scared. The women were all seated while the men stood around staring blankly at each other and the hospital door. The only intermittent distraction was one of the wise men outside, convincing Prakash to go in.

Prakash just wouldn't go in because he wasn't strong enough to deal with the situation. People outside the hospital couldn't fathom the depths of his turmoil. Rita aunty said, "How can he not go in? His father is dying. Doesn't he want to see him one last time?" But Prakash stood in a corner, scared, shaking. Here was a young man who hadn't been scared of anything his whole life. Yet, he was now faced with the scariest situation imaginable. The man Prakash depended on for everything in life was on his deathbed and asking for him.

Chand was outside as well. He was still as a statue. His brother, his business partner, his friend was about to leave him. He did not know what to do. He looked at Prakash who was in a dazed state.

Everyone kept calling Prakash inside but he wouldn't go in. Vidya was crying inconsolably and Nima was begging her brother to come and meet his father. But Prakash was shivering because of the shock. How could God think of taking his father away from him? Things would become alright, he hoped. He did not want to go in and face reality.

Finally, Chand mustered the strength, dragged Prakash by the hand and took him inside. Prakash stood staring at his father and could not control himself. He broke down. Manohar looked at Chand and told him, "Take care of him and Nima. He has a lot of responsibility now. He has to get Nima married."

Chand looked at Manohar and said, "Don't worry. I will take care of him. Your legacy will not go wasted."

Manohar smiled and closed his eyes. It was as if he had been waiting to hear these words before he left the material world. The room and everything else around was shrouded in a deep silence. A few crows flew by and their cries marked the departure of a soul; a good man who always lived by his principles and never compromised.

Dharam had lost one of its founding partners.

Bombay Meri Jaan

O Arjuna that which out of delusion you do not wish to perform, you will do unavoidably, being bound by your own inclinations born out of your own nature (18.60).

—Bhagvad Gita

For Prakash, his world had collapsed. For about a month, he did not go to work. Chand left him alone as he knew Prakash needed time to heal.

After a month had passed, Chand met Prakash at his home back in Punjab. Theirs was a very traditional house. There was a hall with a sofa, a recliner and a rickety bed with a mattress over it, a kitchen adjoining the hall and a couple of bedrooms. Even though he was an industrialist, Manohar had lived a simple life. He could have afforded much more but preferred a minimalistic existence. He had moved some of the furniture and some of his belongings to Bombay but some had been left behind.

Chand sat himself on the sofa. It had been a month, but Prakash looked shaken, as if it had happened just yesterday. He was in a corner looking blank and staring at the space in front of him. Chand gave him a glass of water and said, "So, when are you joining us?"

He looked up. "I have a job at Engineers India already, and I'm not sure if I want to go into textiles."

Chand took the glass of water from him and said, "Hmm...So how much money do you make at Engineers India?"

"Well, I make eight hundred rupee per month."

"You've also got a sister whom you have to marry off?"

"Yes."

"How much money does one need for a wedding, Prakash?"

"I don't know. Maybe ten or twenty thousand."

"Hmm...Prakash, my estimate says it takes at least fifty thousand rupees if you want her married into a good family and want to have a decent wedding where all your relatives show up."

"Okay."

"So, that means five years of your salary will be needed for her wedding. That is if you don't spend it on anything else."

"Has my father not saved anything in the company?"

"He has saved more than enough for her wedding. But this example was just to show you how one single event can be so overbearing financially. If your father had not saved money, your sister's wedding would cost you five years of your income. In a business, there is no limit to how much you can earn."

"People progress in jobs as well, uncle."

"You're right and so does the cost of living. In a job, one struggles to have a good life for oneself. If your business clicks, generations are provided for."

"I will not leave my job for money, uncle."

"Okay. I will give you a week to think about it. If your heart is not in it, don't join. I will pay you Manohar's fair share if you decide to continue with your job."

He decided to leave it at that. A good salesman, Chand used to say, knows when to quit convincing. Prakash wasn't going to change his mind that instant.

Before leaving the house, he suddenly turned and said, "You know, before I leave let me tell you this. Today, for the first time I've seen a man and not a boy. I see a man who has responsibility on his shoulders. In your eyes, I saw Manohar and I know you will not let his legacy and dreams die."

A good salesman also exits the stage with a punch line. Chand was quite dramatic. If he were not in textiles, he'd have been in Bollywood. Raj Kapoor was lucky Chand didn't join the film industry.

Prakash started thinking about what he had been told. He had no idea what to do, no idea what he wanted and felt utterly lost. His father had once told him, "You know, Prakash, when you are lost and have no idea about what you're going to do next, that is the moment you really find out who you are and what you are destined for."

He looked up, tears in his eyes, "I miss you, Dad. I don't know what to do here. I really don't. I wish you were here with me."

He thought about it for a couple of days and came to the conclusion that he had to see the business for himself first to make an intelligent decision. He had to do it quickly because pressure from his workplace to rejoin was increasing.

Prakash booked his ticket for Bombay and reached after a couple of days.

He also landed at the famous Victoria Terminus Station, where his father and uncle had stepped down all those years ago. Chand was supposed to come and pick him up but Bombay traffic delayed him.

Prakash was surprised at the crowds. The station was buzzing with people. He had a couple of bags with him and as he stood to take in what he saw, he put them down. Suddenly the guy next to him shouted loudly.

"*Deva Deva Deva.*"

Prakash was stunned and turned to look at him. His eyes left the luggage for a split second. Someone snatched it and started running away. By the time Prakash turned, the guy had vanished with his belongings. Prakash was shocked at what had just happened. He realized he had been duped as the man who had been shouting had vanished as well.

Prakash ran in a random direction to see if he could spot the thief. He started shouting loudly,

"Thieves, thieves…Catch them. Don't let them get away."

The VT station was full of people and he just couldn't spot the man who had run away with his bags. People would give him a glance and keep walking. Bombay didn't care if Prakash had lost his luggage. He was surprised. Back home, a group of people would have gathered by now to help him catch the thief.

Chand reached the station and saw Prakash running like a madman trying to trace his luggage. He ran after him and held him "What happened?"

"My luggage, uncle. My luggage."

"Someone stole it?"

"Yes."

Prakash was in tears. He had been emotionally distraught for the past few days and had hardly come to terms with his father's death. For him, the loss of his luggage was the limit.

Chand hugged him and said, "Prakash, check your wallet. Do you still have that?"

Prakash checked and said, "Yes, I do."

Chand hugged and told him, "Don't worry. Be thankful that you have your wallet. This is a city of deception. What you see around you is never what the truth is."

"Why stay here then? I don't want to. This is a city of thugs."

"Apart from all that, this is also a city of dreams and opportunities. Bombay is a city which deceives and the deception teaches you a lot of things. This city will give you much more than you've just lost. Give it time and you will get used to it. And then you will never want to leave it."

Prakash regained some composure. "My clothes were in there."

Chand smiled. "That's alright. Time you got new clothes, Prakash. Lots of stores here. You are the owner of a factory which makes fabric. Don't be so sad about losing your clothes."

Prakash smiled back. "Let's file a complaint."

Chand told him, "It's useless. Those policemen out there will just end up troubling us. We'll end up paying more than those clothes were worth, especially to manufacturers such as us. Trust me and let this go."

Prakash sighed. Chand then patted him and said, "How much money have you got, Prakash?"

"Not much. I just have fifty rupees."

They started to walk out of VT station. Prakash had never seen a structure like VT before. He was a civil engineer and was enthused by good structures. The look was quite close to the Indian palaces which were home to the kings in 1877 when VT was built and also reminiscent of the Gothic style of architecture prevalent in the medieval period in Europe. Stone domes and pointed arches adorned the station. A high central dome in the centre had a female figure holding a torch in her hands.

Prakash immediately said, "Who is she?"

Chand replied, "She's my second wife. They've put her up there because my first wife couldn't tolerate her."

Prakash smiled. "Seriously, do you know who she is?"

"I don't. Probably someone famous."

Outside, Prakash noticed a couple of vendors selling vada pav. He had heard a lot about the traditional Mumbai dish.

He asked Chand, "Uncle, I want to try that vada pav."

"Go ahead."

Prakash bought a vada pav for himself and happily ate it.

Chand walked to the place where his Fiat was parked. Before sitting inside, he looked at Prakash who was still eating. He smiled and said, "By the way, welcome to Bombay."

When they were seated in the car, Chand said, "You know, Prakash, a lot of famous people here say they came here with ten or twenty rupees in their pockets and ended up with lakhs of rupees because of their hard work. You can now say I came here with fifty rupees and no clothes. Your start will be slightly different."

Prakash smiled. "I have to make it big if someone is to write about my life."

Chand looked at him and smiled. "Something tells me you will."

Chand drove away with Prakash humming the popular song *Aye dil hai mushkil jeena yahan, zara hatke, zara bachke, yeh hai Bombay meri jaan*. (It is difficult to live here, move to the side, save yourself, this is Bombay, my darling.)

This is Not Your Cup of Tea

The mighty chariot warriors will consider that you retired from the battlefield out of fear and for those whom you have been held in great esteem you will fall into disgrace (2.35).

—Bhagvad Gita

Prakash was put up in Chand's house. He lived in a two bedroom flat close to the factory with his wife, son and daughter. The building had seven floors. He had a well-furnished flat which was quite glamorous, unlike Manohar's simple house. There was imported furniture, couches and the décor was pretty magnificent even for those times. He was a businessman who had money to spend and he spent it well.

Sheila served both of them dinner and they went off to sleep. Early the next morning, they straight away went to the factory. When he walked into the shed, people suddenly got up. Prakash wasn't used to this at his earlier workplace and was surprised to see this culture. Guess this was what his friends joked about when they talked about a 'Seth' driven company.

The production team recognized Prakash as Manohar's son and extended the same courtesy that they had shown to him. Since Chand looked after sales, most of the decisions related to production and labour were taken by Manohar. His death had apparently orphaned at least fifty other people apart from Nima and Prakash.

Prakash was surprised at the princely treatment that he was given. Shah, the main technician, came up to him and said, "Sir, your father was a great man. Chand sir told us that it was not sure whether you would decide to come here or not. Either way, we respect the fact that you are his son. Through you we would all get one more chance to express our love, gratitude and respect for Manohar sir."

Prakash stared at Shah and said, "Thank you. I don't understand the business much. I am not even from a textile background. I think I will end up misguiding you all instead of being an asset."

Shah replied promptly, "Manohar sir learnt on the job too and in no time he was telling us technicians what had to be done. You will pick it up. The only decision you have to make is whether you want to stay here. Don't worry about learning the ropes."

It was a very tough call for Prakash to make. The choice was between a steady, secure job and joining a business which was risky. It wasn't an easy decision. He knew nothing of the business and would probably be expected to pick it up at breakneck speed.

So much was going through his mind at that moment and he felt he needed some air. He stepped out of the factory for a while. As he stood there staring at the sky, hoping for some form of divine intervention, he was joined by Chand who had just come back to the factory from a meeting.

Chand went up to him and kept his hand on Prakash's shoulders. "Trying to locate your father?"

"Yeah. It feels very lonely now that he's gone."

Chand sighed. "Prakash, I have spent the last few days trying to convince you to join the business for which your father had struggled very hard. But I also want that you should be happy in whatever you do. So if you derive that joy from your job, you should go with that. Do not feel guilty about the choice that you make."

"I'm not sure, uncle, about what would be the right thing to do right now. This business is my father's legacy. I want to be a part of it, but I am just scared and confused right now."

"Your father wanted you to be happy, always remember that. Maybe this business is meant to come to a close after my death."

Prakash asked him, "Where did Dad stay?"

"He used to stay in the flat next to mine. I didn't show it to you yesterday because you were quite tired. We've kept it locked since his passing."

"This entire cycle of life and death is just so strange. Just a couple of months back he was fighting hard for the firm, for profits and so much more. Now, he's no more. What did he build all this for? He left before he could enjoy the fruits of his hard work. More often than not, one does not always enjoy the fruits of one's own creation."

"My uneducated guess is that he built it for you. Anyway, the process of creation is quite incredible. Manohar enjoyed creating and building Dharam. That satisfaction was his reward."

Prakash looked at him and managed a weak smile.

Prakash went back to Punjab soon. He deliberated over what he had been told for a couple of days. He did not seek any more advice because he realized that he had to make the final call himself. A couple of nights after he had come from Bombay, he was having dinner with his mother and sister.

He said, "We're going to Bombay."

His sister replied, "What?"

"Yeah. I've decided to leave Engineers India and join Dharam."

His mother, Vidya, was happy that he had taken this decision. His sister Nima was supportive of whatever decision Prakash took.

Nima asked him, "What prompted you to take this decision?"

"When I went to Dharam, I realized this is what father had worked for all his life. He built a legacy, a dream. So many people were dependent on his decisions for their livelihood. They respected him. I loved my father and there would be nothing greater than taking his legacy forward."

"What about your dreams? You wanted to be an engineer, didn't you?"

"I will. I will construct, build, design, if not for Engineers India, then for Dharam. I will not build refineries, I will build textile factories. There is a limit only if you set it. This is also an opportunity to learn something new."

"If you've made your decision then I'm with you 100 percent."

Prakash conveyed his decision to Chand. He was more than happy to accept Prakash as part of the firm.

Prakash left for Bombay after resigning from EIL and serving his notice period. He decided to first go there alone until he had some firm footing in the company. He started going to the production unit and made an earnest effort to learn the process.

Even though Prakash was well educated, he was new to the field. Chand wanted him to learn the ropes from Shah before he took any major decision. Shah was the boss in a way and Prakash the apprentice.

Prakash committed mistakes, ones which were expected of a newcomer. Chand was hard on him and reprimanded him in front of Shah. For Chand, business was not a matter of emotions and Prakash had to pick up fast if they were to survive. There is an old saying that when you try to take one step forward, some forces of nature would try to pull you back so that you don't succeed.

For Prakash that challenge came in the form of Shah. Shah had been hired and trained by Manohar and he had a lot of respect for the man who had been his mentor, but at the same time, Shah did not miss any opportunity to earn a quick buck.

When Shah had met Prakash for the first time, he had convinced him to come and join Dharam, but behind the emotional reasons, there was an ulterior motive. Shah had never wanted Prakash to gain too much prominence at the firm.

With Prakash still learning the ropes of the work, Shah had become the new manager of the factory as Chand did not take any interest in the production part of the work. Everything from production to costs was now under his control. Every voucher was signed by him, even though officially Prakash was a partner at the firm.

When Manohar had been in charge, Shah had had no power since he had been answerable to Manohar. But Prakash was a new guy who according to Shah did not know what he was doing and he wanted to use this to his advantage.

Greed controls us all and manifests itself into corruption when given the opportunity. Corruption can eat into any firm if it is not confronted at the right time. Shah got opportunities to over invoice stores and spares and he took it. He shared the bounty with shopkeepers who over invoiced for him. With no one checking him, he was out of control. He was getting richer by the day and his salary was just a small part of his overall income.

Costs started to escalate. Chand realized there was something fishy going on and he told Prakash to sign the vouchers. Shah started to convince Prakash to sign expense vouchers which were quite unreasonable, telling him the factory would work without them and then he would be answerable to Chand for the loss of production.

Prakash came under pressure initially but later on started to put his foot down. He would talk to shops and find out the market rates of spares and started to gradually tighten the noose around Shah's neck.

Shah's attention started to divert towards his add-on income and ways to maintain it. He started to commit mistakes and put the blame on Prakash. He wanted Prakash to go back. Prakash tried to resist but more often than not, because of his inexperience, he would come under Chand's axe. Things started to deteriorate fast.

An entire beam of cloth* went wrong. Shah blamed Prakash for the loss. Chand lost his temper and shouted at him, "What the hell is

---

* A beam of cloth is the run-length on the machine which is typically more than 500 metres of fabric.

wrong with you? Why can't you concentrate? You are nothing like your father. You are useless. I made a huge mistake getting you here." He did not give Prakash an opportunity to explain.

Prakash said, "It's not my fault. Shah decided the design."

"So what the hell were you doing? Couldn't you check? What do you do here?"

Prakash was demeaned in front of the workers. He went to his office and sat down in a daze. He felt insulted and hurt. What seemed rosy from the outside was actually a world full of thorns. He began to feel as though it was the worst decision of his life to leave his job and join Dharam.

This continued for a while and Chand started to lose his patience. The final nail in the coffin was when Shah raised his voice and told Prakash in front of Chand and the other workers, "Sir, you were right. You should go back. This is not your cup of tea."

Prakash looked at Chand and expected him to come to his defence but Chand did nothing of the sort. Shah had succeeded in driving a wedge between Chand and Prakash.

Nautanki – The Drama Begins

Let a man raise himself by his own efforts. Let him not degrade himself. Because a person's best friend or his worst enemy is none other than his own self (6.5).

—Bhagvad Gita

Prakash went and talked to Chand. "I can't do this."

Chand asked him, "So you're giving up?"

"Yeah. This is hell. I don't seem to do anything right. The harder I try, the worse it gets. Your Shah makes it tougher for me. I haven't made most of the mistakes you've shouted at me for."

"Hmm. Listen I know I am hard on you. But things are getting out of hand."

"It isn't me. It is Shah. That man is fleecing you and from the time that I've tried to stop him, he's been after me."

Chand sighed. "I know but what do I do? I don't have any option. He is more experienced than you are. The labourers support him as well. I can't just fire him. The entire shop-floor will be disturbed."

"I don't know. I feel that Shah is using my inexperience to manipulate me. I don't know the cost of hardware items, electrical instalments, etc. When I find out, he puts pressure on me. I know I am being used. There's Shah and then there's you. If there's a mistake, you assume I've made it." He then took a pause and managed a smile. "By the way, I have not started working according to you so how the hell am I the one making mistakes?"

"You have started working. It's just that you are not working well enough. Even if Shah is corrupt, what do you think we should do?"

"For a while, you need to shift me out and I'll focus on something else. You handle Shah directly. Meanwhile I'll find out what Shah is doing."

"What will you do?"

"I've realized in the time that I've been here that there is money in yarn. A texturizing** machine might not be costly for us at this stage. Let's invest in yarn. We'll use what we can in house and sell the rest."

"He'll find flaws with your yarn."

"Shah will not be involved in the yarn division. I'll recruit a separate technician for that. That technician will tell him what's wrong and right with his fabric. I need someone on my side who can talk to the labourers here and let me know what's going on. I need someone aggressive and who can align the labourers with himself so that I can replace Shah."

Chand gave the proposal some thought. He knew the investment had prospects because he had heard that there was good money in texturizing. There was also enough free space in the factory for a texturizing machine. Chand had invested in space with an intention to expand. He had put his investment plans on hold after Manohar's death but he thought he should give Prakash's idea a try.

"Okay. Go ahead."

Prakash scouted around for a texturizing machine and made the arrangements for the installation of the same. As soon as he found a suitable machine, he invested and installed a texturizing unit in the premises. Luckily, there was just enough space in the premises to do

---

** Machine for the conversion of polyester oriented yarn to usable polyester yarn.

it. Shah was surprised at what was going on. He started joking about Prakash behind his back. "This man could not understand fabric. So, he's going to a whole new level. How can Manohar's son be such an idiot?"

Prakash started scouting the market for yarn technicians. He interviewed a lot of people and liked one in particular whom he called for an interview. The man turned out to be very tall, slim and had a huge moustache which he liked to caress. He wore spectacles which did not quite fit and that was the only aspect that probably differentiated his look from that of a ruffian.

"Hello, good morning, sir. I am here for the interview for a yarn technician."

"Yes. Good morning. Please take a seat. What is your full name again?"

He caressed his moustache "Jha…Mahashankar Jha"

"Are there two Jhas in your name?"

"No. There is only one Jha." He smiled "One is enough."

"You're from Bihar, aren't you?"

"Yes. I'm from Bihar, the king of states."

Prakash smiled at him. "Do you really think that Bihar is the king of states?"

Jha's eyes widened and he said with a sly smile, "You don't? Of course, it is the king of states. Bihar has given India everything – crime, politicians, Shatrughan Sinha and..." He paused for a while and caressed his moustache again, "Mahashankar Jha."

Prakash couldn't help laughing. "Yes, yes, of course. What do you know about texturizing?"

"I can run the machine, sir and yarn produced by me is the best. You can make the best possible fabric out of it."

"You're quite confident."

"Yes, sir. That is because I am the best. If there is any defect in the fabric, it is only at the fabric level. If there is any fault in the yarn, it is because of the raw material. If there is no fault of anyone else, it is still not my fault. It is never going to be my fault."

Prakash was slightly confused, "What?"

"Sir, I will never agree to my fault so you will never have to pay claims or damages."

Prakash laughed. Jha had a swagger about him that would have irritated a few people but Prakash hired him. He liked this Shatrughan Sinha duplicate a lot. He needed someone to stand up to Shah, someone who could hold his own.

The first day that Jha entered the premises, he came in with Prakash.

Shah walked up to the both of them. "Prakash, who is this?"

"He is Mahashankar Jha, the head of the yarn department."

"You did not tell me that you were hiring a new head."

Jha meanwhile looked at Prakash, pointed at Shah and said, "Who is this man?"

"He looks after fabric for us."

"Oh. This fabric manufacturing is useless. It is a loss-making process. You are not as useful to this company as I am."

Shah was shocked for a moment. A new recruit had just trashed him and his entire department in front of Prakash. He raised his voice in anger, "How dare you?"

Jha responded back with indignance, "Don't you dare raise your voice. I will shut it down." He then caressed his moustache again.

Shah backed off for a moment. Prakash looked at Shah and raised his hand as if to say, "Stay calm, Shah." For Jha, Shah was too insignificant to matter.

Chand came to meet Jha. Prakash informed Jha who Chand was apriori so that he would not treat him the way he treated Shah.

As soon as Chand came close, Jha fell at his feet. "Sir, you are like my father. It feels as if I have found my father again. I am lucky to be a part of your company. Please give me your blessings."

Chand lifted him up, gave Prakash a smile and said, "Son, welcome to the team. Hope you will earn us a lot of profits while you are here."

Jha smiled and pointed at Shah, "Sir, I will make up for everything this man is losing."

Chand was stunned at the reply. He saw the confidence in Prakash's eyes and thought recruiting Jha would be worth at least to get Prakash in shape.

After Chand's meeting with Jha, Shah met up with him. He told Chand, "I don't think this man is trustworthy. We should get rid of him immediately."

Chand stared at him for a while and said, "I don't think so. Who are you to decide who we keep and who we don't? He is not from your department, Shah. Stick to your job."

Before Shah left, Chand said in a stern voice, "Don't mistake this investment as a diversion of Prakash's interests. He will continue to be involved in fabric and will sign all the expense vouchers himself." Shah quietly walked away without responding to Chand.

Jha was good at what he did and he got the texturizing machine fully functioning within a week of its arrival. Prakash immediately ordered raw material for the machine and handed over the operations to Jha. He asked Jha to keep stock of the raw and finished material. He himself maintained a strict ledger for monitoring costs so that he could capture the profits of this operation.

The operation turned out to be very profitable and gave Dharam the impetus it needed. More importantly, it gave Prakash due respect and a place in Dharam. Shah still tried to blame Prakash for mistakes that were committed. Jha would show the profits of his operation to Chand to balance out the negative effect of Shah's claims. He would give due credit and respect to Prakash openly, much to Shah's annoyance. Chand realized Shah was playing games with him. Courtesy of the yarn department, Prakash started to find his feet in the firm.

While Chand had started realizing that Prakash had a lot of potential, Prakash was still restless. He wasn't satisfied and wanted to take control of the fabric business and for that, he needed Shah out of the way. He remembered Shah's statement. It was like a thorn pricking him continuously. He wanted to taste vengeance by personally evicting him out of the factory. There was something that he had been saving to say to Shah for a long time. He knew that Chand also wanted Shah out but he wanted no disturbance in the operation so Prakash was fore-warned from doing anything drastic.

Chand noticed the profits in the yarn department soaring sky high and called Prakash to the office. "Finally, Manohar's blood has shown its true worth."

Prakash looked at Jha who was working outside, "With some help from someone."

Chand smiled. "Where the hell did you get this nautanki?"

"By luck and the grace of God." He then looked at Shah from the glass partition in his office. He turned to Chand and said with a serious expression on his face, "The drama, uncle, has just begun."

The Dream Team

Your enemies will speak many malicious and insulting words discrediting your prowess. What can be more painful than that? (2.36).

—Bhagvad Gita

Prakash made a plan to get Shah out of the way. He knew it would be a challenge since Shah had been with the company for a long time, but he had his socks pulled up.

The stand-off between Shah and Prakash was increasingly becoming apparent. It seemed that Jha and Prakash were on one side and Shah was on the other side, which made matters worse.

Every voucher that Prakash signed for Shah, Jha had an opinion to give. He would tell Prakash, "This is too high a cost for a tube light stand. This man is a thief." He said this in front of Shah. Shah would get agitated and once or twice even threatened to hit Jha but he was unnerved.

"A thief is a thief and needs to be called thus." Prakash latched on to the opportunity and started slashing Shah's expense vouchers. Things were changing and changing fast.

Prakash realized one thing during all the time that he spent working with yarn. Technically fabric was supposed to have a higher margin of profit than yarn. But at Dharam, the story was reversed. Thanks to Shah's interventions, fabric showed much less profit than yarn, and this irked Prakash.

He went up to Chand and said, "Are you happy, uncle with how things are progressing?"

"Yes. You have done very well with yarn. But I am not happy with fabric."

"So you know it wasn't me who failed in fabric."

"Yes, I realize that now. But the question is what do we do about it?"

"I think it is time you concentrated on sales. I'll focus on fabric production."

"You're going to take Shah out, aren't you? Make sure you have a replacement else things will stop."

"Don't worry. I think I have just the man."

"Hmmm... The apple has far surpassed the tree, I can see."

"No, the blood is the same. It is just that mine is boiling because of my age, so I push myself harder."

Prakash did not want to fire Shah unceremoniously. He wanted to make it look as if it were Shah's fault. Shah had a hold on the labour and any rash move would lead to the labour rallying behind Shah and that would leave Dharam in a spot of bother.

Prakash was deep in thought when Jha walked up to him "What are you thinking about, sir?"

"Nothing."

"Sir, whatever is worrying you, let me know. I will solve everything for you. If you are depressed, since I am working with you, I am depressed as well. Why are you making me unhappy? Tell me what is bothering you?"

"I want to remove Shah."

"So remove him."

"Not without grounds."

"You want grounds?"

"Yes."

"Done. It is very simple. You should come with these problems to me. We are Biharis and we learn politics before we learn to speak our name."

"Okay, but we also have to take due care that the labour working in the fabric section does not turn against us."

"That might be a bit difficult, sir."

"Jha, I can't risk having to replace the entire team. The loss of production would be huge. We will not be able to complete our orders on time."

"You can't be held hostage like this."

"No, I can't. But I can't break away from my situation in whatever way I want to and then assess the damage later."

"Let me try and influence the workers."

It was almost impossible for Jha to influence the entire team. He tried talking to a couple of them about their loyalty to Shah without insinuating anything about taking him out and realized a number of them were firmly behind Shah. He continued the exercise and was able to identify about 25 percent of Shah's team that would possibly stand behind him.

He went up to Prakash. "We have to do something about this."

"How many workers will stay back if we fire him?"

"Maybe 25-30."

"If you can get half the team to stay back, that would be an achievement."

"Let's implicate him in over invoicing. Maybe, the loss of respect will convince a few more to stay."

"Now your political head's started working. Okay, let me search for someone who can get some people along with him. I had met this one man, Sanjay. He seemed quite impressive."

"Yes. I'm quite excited. It feels like we're into serious politics now."

Prakash smiled. Jha befriended a man in the weaving section and promised him a couple of hundred rupees if he could come up with some dirt on Shah. Prakash, meanwhile, started searching for options.

Prakash called Jha a few days later and told him. "It's time we throw him out. I've finalized my terms with Sanjay."

"He has a team with him?"

"Well, not an entire team but he's convinced a few floor supervisors and a quality checker will join us. We will face some escalated costs and loss of production. However, seeing Shah's back is worth it."

"Okay. Let's do it."

"Did you find any grounds that I can use for his ouster in the last few days, Jha?"

"I think Shah has got some major repairs done on the motor. He has paid Rs. 100 and charged you Rs 200. He gave the supplier Rs 20 extra to get a bill of 200 from him. He hasn't got the voucher signed from you yet but he will do so soon. You need to call the supplier and ask him the rate of repairing our motor and he will tell you Rs 100. Shah might argue that the repair work was more complicated but the shopkeeper will tell you he has been paid only Rs 100."

"Why will the shopkeeper agree to this?"

"Well, he has been told that we know about this and we are filing a police case. We are also going to return his material and hold all bills."

"Didn't he call to verify this with Shah?"

"I told him to do so at his own peril. I convinced him that Shah was on his way out. If he wanted to continue business with Dharam, get his previous payments released and not go to jail, he was better off doing away with Shah. I then gave him your number and told him to cross check if he did not believe me."

A few days later, Shah came to Prakash to get all the vouchers signed. As soon as he presented the motor repair bill, Prakash shouted at Shah, "Rs 200 for motor repair! You are fleecing me."

"No, I have not fleeced you, sir. You are unnecessarily accusing me. You've been after me since the day Jha joined."

"Shah, let's talk to the shopkeeper."

Shah immediately realized something was wrong when Prakash said this. Prakash made that suggestion a tad too early. That immediately sent Shah a warning signal that something was amiss and the shopkeeper was probably part of some grand scheme against him.

Shah made an angry face and in a sombre voice said, "Why? You don't believe me, sir."

"No, I don't. You've cheated me, Shah."

"Sir, if you want to take me out of the firm, please do that. But don't question my integrity and reputation."

By now, Shah had realized he was on his way out. The drama was basically a part of a plan to convince his team to stay back. He was also raising his voice. Prakash's cabin had a glass door and it wasn't thick enough, so everything that was being said was audible outside.

Jha was quietly listening outside Prakash's office. He realized Prakash had made a colossal error in bringing up the shopkeeper too early. Preferably, Shah should have been the one who should have called the shopkeeper.

Prakash told him, "If you're so honest, why shouldn't I call the shopkeeper to verify?"

"Sir you've probably told the shopkeeper to lie."

"Are you calling me a liar?"

"Sir, I am not calling anyone anything. In this case, it seems as if the shopkeeper is part of a plan to throw me out."

"There is no plan to throw anyone out. You are, however, accusing your boss."

"You are not my boss, sir. Chand and your father were my bosses. You are a nobody."

"How dare you say that? You are a good for nothing thief. Get out of my sight and my company. I will file a police case with the shopkeeper and will keep this bill as proof that you have committed fraud. Let me now show you how an educated man responds to bullshit."

Prakash didn't call the shopkeeper. However, their tactic of roping the shopkeeper in at the very least prevented Shah from calling him. That would have been a natural defence.

Jha dramatically opened the door and barged into the conversation. He went in and left the door open. He went in and starting shouting "Thief! Traitor! Liar! We should hand you over to the police."

A few workers gathered outside the door. Prakash took the opportunity and raised his voice to the maximum decibel so that everyone in the factory could hear. "You ingrate, you thief. You're a liar. You don't deserve to be in the company. You've been doing this right from the start and costing the company thousands of rupees. I will take you to the police today. They will beat you up and get my money back."

Shah was shocked at Prakash's opportunistic outburst and shouted back, "Sir someone has set me up. Jha and you have something to do with it."

Jha was waiting for this. He slapped Shah on the face, "How dare you accuse me? Give him to the police, sir. I have proof. There is someone from the weaving team who saw this transaction."

Shah was shocked that he had just been slapped in front of the workers. He was also surprised to hear that someone from the weaving team had seen him and ratted on him. Jha had bluffed and it somehow worked because Shah was rattled and did not want a case against him.

Shah quietly said, "Sir, I want to talk to Chand sir."

Prakash told him, "No need. He handles marketing. As far as you are concerned, I am the final decision maker."

Shah realized he was beaten and said, "Then, I will quit. However, my team will leave with me."

"Let's ask them who they want to side with. Call them one by one and we'll ask them to choose between you and us. Whoever says he wants to leave with you is welcome."

"That's fair."

Jha immediately arranged for the weavers, supervisors and technicians to line up.

Prakash came out and explained the situation. "Mr. Shah is leaving us for some reasons. We would like you to decide whether you want to continue at Dharam or leave."

The team was shocked at this sudden development. They had to make a major decision in a matter of seconds.

Prakash wanted them to choose immediately. If they waited for Shah to convince them that their future was secure with him, they would lose a majority.

There were 100 people in Shah's team. They came in one after the other in Prakash's office and made their choice. The net score was 60-40 in favour of Shah.

Even though they lost 60 team members, Prakash and Jha were quite happy because they had expected only 30 people would stay back. Forty was a decent number.

After the drama was over, Shah went back to his desk, collected his stuff and was ready to leave the firm. When he was leaving, he noticed a man outside. He had seen him before working with Vardhan textiles. He immediately realized that the man outside was his replacement.

While leaving, Shah gave Jha a piercing look.

Jha smiled back and said, "Mr. Shah, can you not have one last picture with us? I have got a camera. For old time's sake!"

Prakash looked at him in amazement as he fished out a camera. Jha had the audacity to take a snap. Shah left the firm fuming.

The man outside was Sanjay Lal Hira. Just like Jha, he was supposedly very good at his job. This man had a reputation in the market for being honest, upright and very strict. He was a Punjabi and was quite well built. Sanjay was fearless and a scary proposition for the labourers.

He had been waiting outside and had been told to enter when he would see Shah leaving. Prakash was eccentric that way. He wanted both events to happen simultaneously. He wanted Sanjay to enter and Shah to leave at the same time. It was supposed to signify a change over at Dharam, a new lease of life.

Just before Shah was about to leave, Prakash looked at Shah and shouted out, "That man was not good enough for Dharam. Liars don't deserve a place in an honest company such as this. That man was my father's biggest mistake."

He had exacted his revenge.

Sanjay was an expert and in no time, caught on to Shah's job. He was able to get a few more people to join and in no time, there were 75 people in the fabric team. There was a loss of production because of labour shortage but, as expected, expenses shot down a lot. Dharam's margins, post Shah, grew stronger and Prakash's position in the firm got firmly cemented.

Meanwhile, Prakash clarified everything that he did not understand from Sanjay. He went a step further and asked questions which surprised Sanjay. "Why don't we operate it in this manner. Won't it lead to better results?"

Sanjay started challenging himself and realized Prakash's out of the box thinking was very helpful in optimizing production. Prakash's expertise in fabric and yarn was growing rapidly.

Within six months, Dharam's costs went down by half and efficiency shot up from 60 to 80 percent. Dharam's fortunes had changed. Chand was elated and looked at Prakash with pride.

Prakash, Mahashankar Jha and Sanjay Lal Hira – Dharam's dream team was in place.

The Wife in this Relationship

Following each his own activity, a man finally achieves perfection (18.45).

—Bhagvad Gita

Sanjay's respect for Prakash grew with time. Apart from picking up the technical stuff really well, Prakash was really good at financial management and brought a whole lot to the table.

The relationship between Sanjay and Jha was quite rocky at times. Jha didn't mind Sanjay doing his job but there were multiple instances where Sanjay needed material from Jha. If there was some fault in the material, both men were up in arms against each other.

"You don't know how to manage quality, do you?"

Jha would respond with a swagger in his voice, "My material goes to multiple places. You are not the only user of the material. You don't know how to do your job and always put the blame on me."

"Your material is crappy. For once, accept your fault."

"What fault? There is no fault. The fault lies with you. Jha does not make mistakes."

Sanjay's eyes would widen and grow red with rage. "Jha only makes mistakes. You are worthless and not capable of learning. People like you are spoiling the culture of the company."

Jha would dismiss the conversation and continue his work, "Go talk to Prakash."

It got difficult for Prakash to handle. At times, he would have to physically separate the two because they almost hit each other.

It wasn't always that bad, however. When things were smooth, both would often share a cup of tea with each other and talk as if nothing was wrong between them. Prakash called them 'husband' and 'wife'.

Once, an entire lot of three thousand metres of fabric got damaged. This was unprecedented. Chand was furious but Prakash had got a lot more composed by then. He was used to manufacturing throwing up surprises.

He called Sanjay, "What went wrong?"

"Sir, have you seen the defect?"

"I have, but I would like to know who is responsible for this defect?"

"Seems to me that the basic raw material, i.e. yarn is defective."

"Weren't you able to detect this while the machine was running?" Prakash wanted clarity.

"Sir, it is very difficult to detect that fault at our level. One can only detect it when the material goes for further processing." Sanjay replied honestly.

"Okay. Where did we get the raw material from?"

"Who else, sir? The great Jha."

Sanjay left the room and Jha was immediately summoned. "Yes sir. You called for me?"

"Yes, I did. Jha, there has been a problem."

"What happened, sir?"

"One entire lot of fabric has gotten damaged. We inquired about the base yarn. Turns out we have done the texturizing and clearly there has been a mistake in that process. The mistake seems to be yours. The loss that we have faced is huge."

"Sir, the yarn can't be spoilt. I can't go wrong. I have never gone wrong till now."

"Jha, experience is not a defence for mistakes. The yarn is defective. You want proof of that. Come and see the fabric. You'll come to know whose fault it is."

"Okay sir. Let let me analyze this cutting and I'll get back to you."

"Okay."

Jha took the fabric cutting with him for analysis and studied it for two days. After two days he said, "Sir, there is a mistake in Sanjay's production. It's not my fault."

"Explain."

"See this cutting. My defect will not look like this. This defect is in a straight line. My defects would not have been in a straight line."

"Jha, your defect will only come in a straight line."

"No, sir."

"Jha you may know about the process of texturizing. But you have no idea about fabric production. That error has occurred while making the yarn and not while making the fabric."

"No, sir."

Prakash then raised his voice and said, "Jha, for God's sake accept your mistake. You have gone wrong somewhere. Find out where the mistake has happened and rectify it now."

Jha was taken aback when Prakash shouted. He had not expected this. He walked out of the room and saw Sanjay nearby. He shouted loudly, "He shouted at me for your fault. You are to blame."

Sanjay smiled and said, "You got what you deserve. You're the cause of the huge loss."

Jha heard this and was very angry. He started abusing Sanjay. Sanjay was in no mood to hear abuses. A huge Punjabi man with a large moustache was being abused by a man from Bihar who wasn't even half his size. Sanjay moved towards Jha so as to hit him and set him straight. Jha was bold. His heart was twice the size of his body. He stood there unnerved and kept shouting, "Come...come. Let me show you."

Prakash saw this and immediately intervened. His interference came at the right time, else there would have been a fist fight. Sanjay and Jha backed off, though they continued abusing each other. The workers were watching the ongoing fight with a lot of interest. They were used to this drama.

Prakash knew Jha well by then. He knew Jha would come around. It was difficult to accept that he could be wrong. Jha quietly went away and started looking at the cutting.

He did not come back to Prakash for a few days.

After some time, he approached Prakash. "Sir, I may have been wrong. It seems there has been some mistake with the texturizing process."

Prakash said, "Jha, who'll pay for the loss?"

"Now, let it go, sir. It happens. I will rectify the process and make sure such a thing does not happen again."

Prakash smiled. "You haven't said sorry yet."

"Sorry, sir."

"Good. Now what about Sanjay?"

"What about him?"

"You haven't apologized to him."

"What?"

"*You haven't apologised to Sanjay*."

"You're joking, sir."

"Hmm.... You told him it was his fault when it was not. You abused him at the top of your voice. You need to apologize to him."

"I don't apologize to anyone."

"You apologized to me."

"You are my boss. Who is he?"

"He is a co-worker who you abused for no fault of his."

"No sir. Never."

Prakash gave Jha a disappointed look and said, "Okay."

Prakash didn't force Jha to apologize. He stayed silent on the issue and didn't talk to Sanjay for a few days.

After about a week, Jha did not apologise but he started talking to Sanjay, "So how is the production going?"

"Better than yours."

"How can your production be better than mine? With one machine, I can do what you do with twenty."

"Okay. Jha, go get yourself checked. You're comparing yarn production to fabric. You are not important in the larger scheme of things."

Jha got angry again. But he somehow calmed himself down and teasingly remarked, "Yeah, yeah you're more important than us. We make mistakes. You are perfect. We cause losses while you bring in profits."

"Yeah, you've just caused the company a huge loss."

"I know. How much more pain are you going to cause me for that?"

Sanjay realized Jha was defeated. He had just admitted he was wrong. That was as much of an apology as he was ever going to get from Jha.

He patted Jha on his back. "It happens to the best of us. We all make mistakes."

Jha looked at him and gave him an evil smile. "Yeah, I should not be that depressed. You make more mistakes than me but look at you. You're so happy."

Sanjay laughed and said, "You, Mr. Jha, are never going to change."

He gave Sanjay his Shatrughan Sinha pose with the all so familiar swagger and caressed his moustache, "Jha! Mahashankar Jha. I am perfect. I don't need to change. You on the other hand could bring about some changes in yourself."

"Okay, okay Mr. Perfect. Let's go get that cup of tea. The arrogance does not subside even when you are apologizing."

They came back from that tea break in smiles.

Prakash went up to them and said, "Husband and wife had gone for a cup of tea, I see."

Jha immediately shot back, "Yes, I'd taken my woman out."

Sanjay responded saying, "Jha, look at your size. You are the woman in this relationship."

I am Not Born to Yield

O scion of Bharata [Arjuna], O conqueror of the foe, all living entities are born into delusion, overcome by the dualities of desire and hate (7.27).

—*Bhagvad Gita*

Ever wonder what happens to people at the bottom of the pyramid. The concerns, hopes and dreams change drastically across these layers. It is the lowest at the bottom most layer where life can get so dark, one wonders the futility of being born. There lies the real India, the masses. Uday Shankar Chaubey was one who belonged to the bottom most level and the darkest recesses of the country. He was born in an abyss.

"Uday, come and have your dinner. Come quickly."

Uday had not eaten anything the entire day, yet he shouted back, "Maa, I don't want to have anything. I am not hungry."

His father ranted, "Don't give that good-for-nothing thankless idiot any food if he's not hungry. You never ask your husband if he's hungry. You first check if your good-for-nothing son is well-fed."

His mom suddenly went silent. Her mother-in-law joined in, "You've married an evil woman. This b★★★★ and that b★★★★★★ son of yours are the worst people I know."

Some children are born in hell and Uday Shankar Chaubey was, unfortunately, one of them.

A well-built child, Uday Shankar Chaubey was tall, fair and well-toned. He had quit school after the fourth standard simply because his good-for-nothing father couldn't support his education and he could not bear to see his mother slog. He started working for a small textile mill early on as a helper whose job was to move goods around the factory from one place to the other.

He lived in a small 10"X12" house which accommodated four people – him, his parents and his grandmother. Uday and his mother would often sleep close to each other after his father was done abusing her sexually. His father would throw Uday and his mother out of the house while he raped his wife and would call them back in after he finished.

Even as a child, he could hear his mother scream before his father called them back in. Innocence can turn brazen at an early age if it is driven to the extent that was in this case. His blood boiled but his mother held him back saying this was his father and they had nowhere else to go.

His father was a drunken sloth. He would use his wife's salary for drinks and regularly beat her up. Uday would try and interfere and was able to stop him at times but the abuses would continue. His grandmother also never held back. For her, Uday's mother was to blame for all her troubles. Her son was her fruit and life wasn't rosy. With no one to blame, Uday and his mother were soft targets.

Whenever there was a big fight, Uday and his mother would get away from their father's sight by going to a corner or by leaving the house for a while. His mother would cry and Uday would calm her down. He was quite mature for his age.

There was a small girl Savitri who lived in the same locality and was three years younger to Uday. She was the only one Uday unloaded his heart and soul to. He would cry in front of her when things got really bad and she would often console Uday saying, "Everything will become okay one day." Her parents sympathized with Uday and would often abuse Uday's father behind his back.

Over time, because of his father, Uday became combative. He did not tolerate any nonsense from anyone. He would regularly get into fights and received many warnings from his supervisor. The only reason he was not fired from his job was because he was a strong worker.

There were days he slept without food. He always ensured his mother ate on time. He would look at his grandmother with disgust most of the times because of the way she treated his mother.

His grandmother would often shout out loud, "Savitri, where is my lunch?"

"There isn't enough food for us all."

"Don't feed that son of yours. He is a curse to this house. I want my food."

Uday would move to hit his grandmother but his mother always stood in the way. She offered to give him food and stay hungry herself but Uday never allowed it.

He knew that since his father took away all the money that his mother earned, it was his salary with which the household was running. Uday started to work around the food problems in the house. He started hiding some money away from his father which he would use to quietly take his mother out of the house, feed her and have something himself.

Over time, his father started to realize that Uday was not getting money home. He wasn't as strong as Uday so he got a belt home to try and hit him.

On that fateful day, Uday was supposed to work the night shift. He was home all afternoon. His father came home, completely drunk and with a whip in his hand. His mother saw the whip and was petrified. He shouted loudly, "Come here, you b******. You're hiding money from me, you son of a b****."

His mother was petrified and cried loudly, "Don't hit my son!"

Uday was unmoved. His eyes were red that day as if he was waiting for his father to use that belt. It would take one move from his father with that belt for him to burst.

His father was too drunk to notice Uday's anger. He moved towards Uday and his mother came in between. The leather hit against her skin and she cried out in pain. Tears started flowing out of her eyes and blood started to ooze out of her skin. Despite all this, she did not move away from her son.

Uday saw that and rushed towards his father, held him and slapped him hard on the face. He took the belt from him and hit him four or five times. He took one shot at his father's genitals and his father almost lost his senses. His father was listless with pain and could hardly even shout. His mother moved to stop Uday but he held her with one hand and kept on hitting his father. It was as if years of frustration had culminated into this.

His grandmother was shocked and did not dare to move towards them and threatened Uday, "I will call the police."

Uday took the phone from her hand and hit his grandmother once with the belt albeit with lesser force. She immediately fell on the ground. She started shouting loudly and was weeping inconsolably.

The neighbours started to gather outside the house. His neighbours knew about Uday's father and chose not to intervene. Uday locked the door in case they changed their mind and continued hitting the two of them. They were bleeding profusely. He then looked at his mother and said, "Let us go away from here. There is nothing for us here."

His mother immediately went in and packed whatever little she had. They then opened the door to let the neighbours in and ran away from there. They took a train out of the city. The neighbours did not try to stop them or call the police. Uday's father and grandmother were not in a position to call anyone.

Uday and his mother got into a train to Bombay without any reservation along with their luggage. He was slightly scared while his mother was almost shivering with fear. The train was so crowded that no ticket collector came to check up on them. They managed to make it to Bombay undetected.

Eventually when the matter went to the police authorities, no one testified against Uday. His father and grandmother complained about Uday but Savitri and her parents testified against them. It was too insignificant a case for the police to investigate and died out soon after.

Uday and his mother never found out what happened to their father. For practical purposes, he was dead to the both of them. His grandmother passed away a couple of weeks after they left the two of them. His father had developed liver problems because of his drinking and died soon after.

In Bombay, the first few days for both Uday and his mother were extremely difficult. They were starting a new life, but they had nowhere to go and so the first day, both of them slept on the road. The next day, Uday did some labour work for a construction facility and managed to get some money. He used that for food. He befriended another construction worker, Amar, who offered him and his mother temporary shelter.

Meanwhile, he scouted around for jobs. Luckily in those days, there were jobs available for people who had worked in the textile sector before. He joined a textile mill in Bombay. He got a very small house on rent and started staying with his mother. Given the hell that they had seen back home, a less than ordinary life in Bombay was a blessing.

A lot of people use karma as logic for privilege and it probably is the only explanation however far-fetched. The distribution of privilege among living beings is otherwise just too random. A lot of children his age would be pampered by their parents right in front of him. They cried for not getting the toy they wanted or the sweet they wanted to have. Uday never shed a tear even when he did not have a basic meal. He knew his life would not move an inch if he cried or threw a tantrum. He had to bear the responsibility for himself and his mother.

He would often see school children smiling and playing and would ask his mother "What did they do to deserve that fate and what did I do to deserve mine?"

She would give him a sad smile and say, "You were born in a poor family and that is a disease. We are infected by poverty."

"How do I get out of it?"

"I don't know. The funny thing is that money leads to more money. So, I don't know how these people get loads of it while we have none. We are slaves to these people and have to do what they want. They control everything because of their money – the police, political leaders. They decide when we are allowed to breathe and live."

"I am a slave to no one and will do what I want in life, Maa. I will not yield before people."

"We are born to yield to them, son."

"No, I am not. They have everything today because of the families they were born into. I don't respect them. Had their blood been from a different father, they would be worse than me because none of them have the capacity to work as hard as me."

This attitude defined Uday. He believed he had to ask for forgiveness from no one if he committed no wrong. There was no negotiating with him.

He worked diligently in a yarn factory in Bombay and slowly picked up the art of becoming an operator. They frequently had trouble meeting ends because of the high rentals and by the time the end of month arrived, there was enough food for only one of them. Most of the time, Uday slept without food.

He was not a dreamer. Life had let him down so much that he had made peace with the fact that life was about survival. The only other thing he held on to was his pride. He developed his own sense of right and wrong and never compromised. He was thrown out of multiple jobs because of this. He got into frequent altercations when he thought his supervisor was not being fair to him.

The days when Uday was without a job were the toughest on him and his mother. His mother, however, never complained to him about sleeping hungry. She would cry silently in a corner and it was mostly because her son had slept without food.

She prayed to God to make things right but Uday told her once, "The problem with prayers, Maa, is that you expect God to listen to them and he is supposed to make things right but like everything on earth, he listens intently to the rich and ignores us completely."

However, Uday always managed to switch and get another job courtesy a sharp mind and hardworking demeanour. He grew quickly because of his ability to pick up things and soon commanded the salary of a skilled operator. His salary over time was enough to maintain himself and his mother with dignity.

One thing defined him through all his jobs: "I am not born to yield."

His Eyes Show no Relent

Even a knowledgeable person acts according to his own nature. All living entities are controlled by their own natures. What can repression accomplish? (3.33).

—Bhagvad Gita

Jha found an avenue to expand the yarn department at Dharam. He was always looking for ways to expand his influence in the company. He approached Prakash with this idea "I think we should expand in yarn."

Prakash looked at him and said, "I'm not expanding in yarn."

He then told Jha in a coy tone, "Anyways, yarn is loss making."

Jha blew it. "What? Sir, I respect you but please don't insult me. We Biharis know everything. I know you are making a lot of money because of yarn. Wherever Jha goes, there is prosperity."

"Wherever Jha goes, there's trouble."

Jha got excited when he heard Prakash say this. He immediately shot back, "If you are not expanding the yarn section, I'm leaving."

"Jha, no one else will tolerate your whims. I will do it to a limited extent. Let's get three machines."

"What? Three machines are useless. The other costs will be so high you will make a loss. We should go for seven machines."

"Four."

"Six."

"Five."

"Done."

"My God. I can't believe you just negotiated about the number of machinery."

"See, the things I have to do to make money for you. You must have done something good in your past life."

"Yeah. You're right. No wonder I got Sanjay as an employee. I wonder what crimes I committed to get you."

Jha smiled, "No problem, sir. You get me those machines. I will show you." He then laughed and stroked his moustache "Jha... Mahashankar Jha."

Jha had done the necessary research and had identified potential vendors for the machinery. Prakash got an inspection done and purchased the relevant machinery. Jha and company set up the machinery for yarn processing. The machinery was installed and ready for operation within a month of its purchase. He then searched for operators to run those machines. He was able to line up four operators at first.

The first person to join the twisting operation at Dharam was Ramraj. A thin man, he seemed to be hard working. Jha liked him instantly.

The second operator to be hired was Hawaldar Singh. He was from Uttar Pradesh. A tall, well-built man, Hawaldar Singh was quite an outspoken person. Jha did not like him at first because of the way he spoke but he needed fourteen guys and he needed them quick. Hawaldar Singh was a way to fill a requirement and quickly get started.

At number three was a man named Foudhar Singh. He was related to Hawaldar.

The fourth person was fair, well-built, had a huge moustache which was curled at the ends.

Jha started his interview. "What is your name?"

"Uday Shankar Chaubey."

"Where are you from?"

"Bihar."

"Where in Bihar?"

"Gaya district."

"Hmm okay. What kind of work do you do, Chaubey?"

"Loading these machines. I've operated them before."

"Where?"

"In Mahesh Synthetics. They had a fairly large operation."

"Why did you leave that place?"

"The management was very caustic. They were not fair to me."

"What did they do?"

"They were bad people, sir."

"Hmmm... Were they bad people or were you a difficult person?"

"Nothing like that, sir."

"Okay. You look aggressive. Taper that aggression. It won't work here."

"Okay, sir."

Jha hired ten more people and the twisting operation was more or less set. Avdesh Pandey, Jawahar Lal Shinde, Umesh Yadav, Kranti Kumar, Mohan Singh, Radhe Shyam, Sevak Ram, Om Prakash Yadav, Vinay Pandit and P. Vijay Kumar.

With these operators in place, the twisting setup was ready for operation. There were about one hundred workers in Dharam across different operations when these sixteen operators came in.

The twisting machines were placed at the extreme corner of Dharam. The entire area was now packed. For any further expansion, they would need more space.

Prakash approached Chand. "We should find some more space in Bombay and try to expand."

Chand immediately replied, "Interesting that you talk about expansion in Bombay. But I think it is time to wait and watch."

"Why?"

"There is a man being talked about in the circles of Mumbai. Apparently he is called Doctor Sahab. His influence on the textile workers on Bombay is immense."

"Unions come and go. This union will also disappear with time."

"This man does not look like he is going away that easily. It seems that he might alter the political and the union landscape of the country. The Prime Minister Indira Gandhi has also taken note of his existence and the Congress is backing him."

"Oh! A union leader backed by the leading political party in the country. That can't be good."

"Nope. It isn't. It is worrying. Anyways, let us see how things progress."

They decided to curb expansion and focus on consolidating their operation. They had a fairly steady market. Chand had excellent marketing skills and was able to get good rates for their products in the market.

By 1982, Dharam had expanded quite a bit. They were firmly established in yarn and fabric. Their own production was not enough for fulfilling their market obligations. They started to outsource by supplying raw material to cash strapped firms who couldn't afford to invest in the material and got the manufacturing done by them.

Getting job work done was a pain. Prakash had to handle the stress of both in-house production and job work. He had to manage quality issues along with stock of raw material. It was getting very stressful for him to manage.

Prakash wanted to get more machines in-house and increase production so that he would not have to deal with the hassles of job work accounting and quality issues.

Chand had a different attitude to things. He figured that in-house production should be limited because demand management round the year to feed the in-house looms was difficult and that put a lot of pressure on the firm. Also, he was wary of handling a lot of labour.

Things were rapidly changing around them. The textile circle had started talking about Dr Datta Samant in hush hush tones. Workers had started to rise against their owners and placed their demands in front of their satraps. It was becoming difficult to compete with other textile clusters in India. Land prices were increasing rapidly and it was more profitable to sell the setup than to run it.

The way things were going in Bombay, it was becoming more and more difficult for mill owners to survive. Costs had started to escalate. Waves of trade unions had started sweeping mills one by one. The Bombay textile industry was on the verge of a tsunami…

The Great Bombay Textile Strike

Whichever and however a great man conducts himself common men do also; whatever he accepts as authority that and that alone certainly all the world will follow (3.21).

—Bhagvad Gita

Doctor Saheb was slowly entering the textile firms. The size of his following was increasing and mill owners in Bombay were getting increasingly anxious. Reports suggested that 2,50,000 to 3,00,000 workers were behind him.

The institution of textiles is an old one in Mumbai. In fact, the popular 'pav-bhaji' was a concoction first conceived by Mumbai workers for whom this was a quick meal. It was a mixture of all the traditional curries one ate with bread. It is ironic that one of the most popular dishes in Bombay which is now a favourite across classes came out from the lack of time and from the needs of the poorest sections of society.

Workers were overworked and under paid. Strenuous physical labour ensured that they in fact had little time for lunch. Mill owners used to physically and verbally abuse workers. It was the worst form of capitalism. Dissatisfaction was brewing and there was fertile ground for an agitation.

This frustration among the labour class in Bombay was bound to lead to frustration and animosity between the haves and the have-nots.

A man named Datta Samant (also called Doctor Sahib) took advantage of this frustration. On 18 January 1982, a strike was called by the mill workers of Bombay. They were demanding increased wages and bonuses and wanted the Rashtriya Mill Mazdoor Sangh to be de-recognized as the only official union in the country.

At that time, there were approximately two-and-a-half lakh mill workers who worked in Girangaon, the textile village. Large gatherings of these workers could be seen at various grounds in Bombay.

Dr Samant would address these workers from a dais, stressing on how they had been exploited and how that would not continue in the future. He was their messiah – the solution to all their problems. The mill workers were standing squarely against the mill owners and both sides were in no mood to compromise.

Dharam had not yet been affected by the strike. Work continued as usual. Prakash and Chand were getting worried that they would not be left untouched. They had to do something quickly.

One operator from the twisting operation, Hawaldar Singh came to Prakash. "Sir, I've heard the mill workers across Bombay are going to go on strike. We also want increased wages and bonuses."

Prakash replied, "We are already paying you what the market allows us to. Our salaries are more than most companies."

"I don't care, sir. If you don't agree to our demands, people here are saying they will join the strike and create havoc."

"Are you threatening me, Hawaldar Singh?"

"No sir. I am not threatening. I am just telling you what these workers think." He then paused for a while, "If you want me to bring them on your side, take care of me."

Prakash's eyes were red with anger. "I don't want you to convince them and I do not want to take care of you. Please go back and do your job."

Hawaldar Singh gave Prakash a wicked smile and said, "Think about it, sir. You might regret it." He then took some tobacco out from a packet and started chewing it. "I will come back later."

Prakash immediately summoned Jha and reprimanded him for his choice of operator. "From where did you recruit that idiot, Hawaldar Singh?"

"From nowhere in particular, sir. What happened?"

"He threatened me that the workers might go on strike if I don't increase salaries and bonus or if I don't pay him off."

"What? He said that?"

"Yeah. What do we do now?"

"Why are you panicking? This is an industrial establishment and these situations are common. Only if you learn to tackle these will you be able to run this company."

Prakash raised his voice. "Okay, right now I am in no mood to educate myself on how companies are run. Please get rid of this menace."

Jha realized he could not remove Hawaldar Singh outright. Labour laws were strict in terms of layoffs and the environment outside was very hostile, thanks to Doctor Saheb. There was no easy way of laying Hawaldar Singh off. The other problem was while gratuity was due to workers only after completing five years, some workers had recently started claiming ridiculous amounts if you threatened to remove them. Mr. Samant was always willing to lend any of these workers a helping hand in case they wanted to go on strike.

The great Bombay textile strike was the biggest of its kind in the history of the country. It was unprecedented that Dr. Datta Samant had been able to garner so much support. Even the political parties had to stand up and take notice. The strike was a move to remove the registered union and to grasp power. Unions in those times had unlimited clout. The union leader was at par with the local politicians, in some cases stronger than the politicians. Everyone from politicians to factory owners wooed them.

Prakash visited one of the places in Tardeo where the strike was on. Near the Bombay Textile and Weaving Mills, there was a huge procession with about 75,000 workers listening to Dr. Datta Samant speak about how they were being repressed. There was a dais and a couple of loudspeakers. The mood was of dissent and the atmosphere there was quite grim. Workers were shouting slogans. Traffic access was blocked and vehicles were being diverted. The mill was closed and workers were focused on what Dr. Samant was communicating to them.

Prakash stood there and heard the demands that were being made. Most of the demands in his opinion were reasonable and he was surprised that a few of the practices being demanded for were not being followed in rival textile firms.

Prakash walked away from there and went straight away to Chand's house. Chand had just come home from work. "What happened?"

"It is a huge strike. It will soon engulf all the companies, including Dharam." Prakash told him what he'd seen.

"Are you sure it is that bad?"

"I went to the place where Dr. Datta Samant was addressing the workers. They are in no mood to back off."

"Maybe the mill owners will relent."

"Uncle, the mill owners might not relent. Word on the street is that they are backed by the politicos. Also, most of them were not making that much profit. They will earn much more if the lands are put up for rent or sale."

"Hmm. So what do you suggest?"

"We need to move production out of Bombay."

"That is a big decision. Where do we move?"

"We need to figure that out. We should go anywhere but here."

Chand was silent. It was not an easy task to shift base. The decision would impact machinery as well as labour. There was also the issue of loss of production. Not everyone would be open to moving out of Bombay.

Meanwhile, Hawaldar Singh had started to charm the thirteen people that had joined the twisting operation. They were the most susceptible. The weaving and texturizing operators were relatively older and were attached to Prakash and the firm.

Uday Shankar Chaubey had once asked Jha, "Sir, our salaries are going to be increased, aren't they?"

"Who told you?"

"Hawaldar Singh."

"Hmm. You go back to work and stop talking to that idiot."

Jha realized that he had to do something very quickly. He needed an alibi to chuck Hawaldar Singh out.

Hawaldar was quite an average worker and had never misbehaved in the company. His behaviour changed when he started thinking of himself as the leader of the pack. He would pat workers on the back for no reason, abuse Prakash behind his back on the slightest chance and even got the curls of his moustache pointing upwards. He would proudly slip his fingers on the curls when he talked about worker's rights. The messiah for the workers had arrived. They didn't need to look outside to listen to Doctor Saheb. Their doctor was in-house.

Jha decided to get the workers together and celebrate Holi. Most of them agreed. Hawaldar Singh was looking for an opportunity to increase his influence on the workers so he readily agreed. It was an opportunity for the future 'leader' of workers to celebrate with his patrons.

Hawaldar Singh was a heavy drinker. This fact was well known to everyone who knew him. At the Holi function, Jha organized a decent supply of *bhang* in a garden near the company. The garden was quite large and a decent place to arrange a function. There was a moderate amount of grass in the park and a few trees on the boundary added to the sparse greenery. It was as good a garden as one could get in an industrial area. Jha decorated the garden to make the environment look festive.

The workers drank as much free *bhang* as they could. There were colours thrown all around. The mood was very festive and colourful. It was party time.

In the background, someone played Holi songs from Bollywood movies on a tape recorder. The workers got a small container from somewhere, filled it up with water and colour and dunked each other one by one into the water. Sure enough, in some time all the workers looked like coloured ghosts out of a horror movie. They were drunk and were swaying to the music. A few workers just lay on the grass reminiscing while others danced away, lost to the world.

Hawaldar Singh got drunk as well. He was quite out of his senses. Jha told Hawaldar Singh, "They think of you as their father and guide. You should talk to them. They are all waiting to be addressed by their future leader."

Ordinarily, Hawaldar would have seen through this blunt stint that Jha was trying to pull. However in this case, he was quite drunk and unable to reason so he got up to address his followers. He shouted loudly,

"Listen up."

Jha started smiling. This had been carefully planned. He had instigated some workers who were his staunch loyalists to make full use of the situation.

The drunk workers turned to look at Hawaldar Singh who started his speech. "I have decided to fight for your cause with the management. We want them to increase our salaries and bonuses and if they don't, we will not work or let anyone work in Dharam."

One of the workers in the group was Jha's loyal aide who worked in texturizing. Kanta was dark and huge. He was so scary looking that not many people had the guts to go against him. Kanta was Jha's go to man if he wanted anything done.

Kanta immediately shouted back, "Who gave you the right to tell us what to do? Who are you anyway? Some new idiot. What do you know about us to represent us? You b*******."

Hawaldar Singh went crazy when he heard Kanta abuse him. He moved to hit him and slapped Kanta. Kanta was not one to take it lightly. He hit Hawaldar Singh and hit him hard. Hawaldar Singh was on the floor. Kanta then started to kick him and Hawaldar Singh yelped in pain. Kanta's aides also joined in to hit Hawaldar till he started to bleed.

Hawaldar Singh lay unconscious on the floor. Apparently, not many people were happy with his condescending behaviour so no one came forward to save him. The few friends that Hawaldar Singh had managed to make were too drunk to care.

Jha then quietly took the workers away. The next day, Hawaladar Singh went to Dharam's office in anger. He had apparently had to go to the doctor himself.

He straightaway went to Jha and said, "I want justice. Dharam has to give me justice."

"For what?"

"For the workers hitting me like that."

"We can't control the workers. They are all saying you abused them and started hitting first."

Hawaldar's eyes widened to such an extent, Jha felt they were going to come straight for him. "What respected co-worker? Kanta's a b★★★★★★. They're all liars and you know it."

"Don't you dare say anything about Kanta, else I'll hit you so hard you will get a one-way ticket to UP."

"Why should I work in a company where no one respects me? They will hit me again."

"That is your choice. If you want to leave, leave now. I agree with you. It is not good to work in a company where you're not respected."

"I will leave. Please give me my dues."

Jha was waiting for that. He immediately prepared Hawaldar's dues and handed them to him. The laws were not that generous if the worker himself offered to quit. His final takeaway was just the pending salary. Hawaldar accepted the final settlement quietly and signed the voucher which sealed his exit.

Jha told him, "Now, listen up. If I see you around Dharam, the animal in me will take over. I will parcel you back to Bihar."

It was quite comical when Jha said that as he was half the size of Hawaldar Singh. Yet, when he said it and looked in Hawaldar's eyes, Hawaldar looked scared. Sanjay, on the other hand, was smiling from a distance. He was used to Jha's empty threats.

Prakash knew that Dharam needed to move as the hostility among the workers in Bombay was likely to create multiple issues in the days to come. It would become impossible for them to operate if they got caught in the eye of the storm.

Prakash had to find another location for Dharam. He had his eyes set on a place called Vasantgam in Gujarat. Gujarat was a rapidly growing state and Vasantgam was well connected to Bombay. There was a GIDC (Gujarat Industrial Development Centre) where lands were available at bonanza prices. He took three days off from Dharam to scout around the place and see if there was a suitable location for his setup.

By the start of 1983, the strike situation in Bombay had worsened. Huge numbers took part and the participation led the workers to believe that they were close to getting their demands met. Most mill owners had decided to take it to the finish. With their financial capability, they were more likely to last any closure than the workers. Politicians realized that a successful strike would lead to the creation of a new power bloc headed by Datta Samant and that further went against the strike.

The strike was getting more and more deep-rooted and there seemed to be no solution in sight. The island city was set to lose its position as the nation's manufacturing hub.

The loser in this case was the average worker who lost his means of livelihood in the process. A lot of them did not want to be part of the movement but were threatened verbally and even physically if they dared to move away from the striking group. Houses went without food and hungry, crying children were a common sight outside them.

The mill owners didn't care. For them, this was an exit from Bombay. Some did not even want to remain in textiles because it was not as lucrative as property. It was better to sell off their mill land and enter construction or some other similar field.

Whenever there is a mass movement of this sort, people lose sight of the purpose and the participants end up being pawns in the hands of those who wield power and money. They become hostage to greed, politics and are just a number to both sides. Their lives are of little significance and even if a few die, they are held as examples by both sides and the game continues.

The Shiv Sena was of the opinion that the strike was affecting the Marathi mill workers and their jobs. As a result, they also protested against Dr. Samant.

Datta Samant however was not willing to relent. The strike was, on paper, over in 1983 without any solution. The mill lands would give way to malls much later and the mill owners were in due time more than compensated for their losses. Millworkers however did not find jobs for years to come.

Some people have an effect on generations to come. Dr. Samant was one of them. He altered the face of the city we now know as Mumbai. Political undercurrents and public emotion in the island city was at a feverish high. The status quo was not even a choice for the workers after a while. Goons blocked the few who dared to protest to end the agitation and mill owners disowned them.

The social and cultural impact on the city was huge. A noted underworld don, Arun Gawli was the son of a textile mill worker and most of his boys were the sons of the second generation locked out textile mills. The 'textile village' was left with dilapidated houses of directionless textile workers left jobless. They tried to regain their lost status time and time again by aligning with political forces but over time became a 'forgotten' lot. Bombay moved on to house financial and service based companies leaving these workers in a lurch.

Mill lands would become bowling alleys and entertainment centres in the years to come. One of them would go on to house the most popular mall the city was to see. The Bombay mill culture was ruined and the silent protests of the mill worker vanished from the island city.

The Great Bombay textile strike changed Bombay forever.

A New Beginning

One cannot remain without engaging in activity at any time, even for a moment; certainly all living entities are helplessly compelled to action by the qualities endowed by material nature (3.5).

—Bhagvad Gita

Gujarat was relatively undeveloped back in the 1980s. It was a risky move to start something there but Prakash was fast running out of options and time; the logical choice seemed to be Vasantgam. They had decided to sell off the factory in Mumbai and use the proceeds from the sale to make an investment in land in Gujarat and a decent office space in Mumbai.

Vasantgam, at that time, was less of an industrial area and more of a developed jungle in many ways. Cows would come out of nowhere if you were driving on the road and you would find cow dung at random places.

There was greenery all around. Huge trees, thickets and undeveloped roads made it a typical Indian village. It was common to spot snakes around the area. You would also find young women with pots filled with water going home.

The village did however have decent drainage facilities and courtesy the enterprising nature of the Gujaratis, was quite clean.

The government had created a separate industrial area for companies. If one stepped into the industrial area, you could see a city embedded inside a village. It was quite a radical combination – the serene, slothful life of a village contrasted with the busy, industrious and focused life of an urban industrial centre.

Prakash had invested in a shed. The shed needed some cleaning and then all the looms could be easily shifted there. The process would take a lot of time and he first needed his key lieutenants, Jha and Sanjay, to be comfortable with the idea of moving to Vasantgam.

He bought Sanjay and Jha along with him to see the village by road. They took Prakash's Maruti Suzuki along with them. The model had been launched a year earlier. It was the '*in*' car to own in those days and was gaining popularity just like the Bajaj scooter the decade before. It was a compact car with a good mileage and decent pickup. The front face of the car looked like a geek wearing spectacles but youngsters were gung-ho about it.

One aspired to own a Maruti and if there was an air conditioner that went along with it, you were probably a businessman or a film star. Prakash fitted into the former category so he had an AC in his Maruti. It wasn't really meant for long drives but in those days there weren't many options.

It was a five hour drive from Bombay, and Prakash had two bickering men sitting behind.

Sanjay commented almost immediately when he saw the village "This is a jungle. You've brought me to Jha's home."

Jha stared at him and then curled his moustache again "Yeah. The lion lives in the jungle."

Sanjay gave him a disgusted look. "When I think of you, I think of wild pigs."

Jha was enraged when he heard this. "Who are you calling a pig?

Prakash broke off their bickering by telling them, "Shut up, both of you. I'm going to take you to the industrial area. That is very much like a city."

Sanjay quipped "Oh, so there is a city. I thought you are going to bring us here and feed us to the lions."

Prakash was not amused by Sanjay's reaction and glared at him. Jha continued, "You have to leave this village woman back in Bombay, Prakash. He can't handle it here."

Sanjay and Jha continued squabbling, much to Prakash's dismay. When they finally reached the industrial area, Sanjay and Jha were quite surprised. There were a couple of residential areas as well and Prakash was thinking of buying land to construct a small building where Sanjay, Jha and the other technicians could reside.

There were about 10 to 15 factories in the area in about 1000 square metre-plots each. It wasn't a chemical zone so there was no pollution in the area. There was greenery in parts and the roads were fantastic.

They were outside Prakash's proposed plot when Jha said, "So, this is where we are going to be?"

"Yeah. Excited?"

Sanjay said, "Not really."

"Sanjay, it is difficult to operate in Bombay and this seems to be a more viable option."

"Where will we stay?"

"Here. I'll come two-three times a week. Initially, I'll come more if needed."

Jha strolled around the area for a while and stroked his moustache. "No problem. We are going to rule this village."

Prakash looked at him and winked, "Jha, you're a king. You rule wherever you go."

Jha smiled. Sanjay was a bit pensive, "I don't know if I can live here."

Prakash put his arm on Sanjay's back, "Tell you what, Sanjay. Initially, I won't force you. You travel here as I do. There are trains which stop here which start from Bombay. If you get comfortable here, you can stay here, else we'll both travel."

"That sounds okay."

"Great."

Jha looked at him and gave a wicked smile. "Prakash sir can't stay here. He has to be in Bombay where his Sushma is."

Prakash stared at him with shock. "How the hell do you know about Sushma?"

"Hmm... You think I don't keep track of your life. I am the all-knowing messiah."

"Yeah, right. Please don't tell Chand about it right now."

Jha immediately shot back. "I won't if you tell us about her."

Prakash spoke with a slight shyness in his voice and a twinkle in his eyes. "I met her through a relative and fell head over heels over her when I saw her for the first time. When she smiles, it feels as if you are rid of your worries. She has a habit of gently touching her hair and she looks like a cute child when she does that."

Sanjay and Jha listened intently. They smiled and Jha patted Prakash on the back and said, "Sir, she is lucky to have met a guy like you."

Prakash smiled.

Jha then asked him, "Okay. Are you going to call this unit Dharam only?"

"Yeah, I am going to go with Dharam. It has a lot of meaning, chief among them being religion, duty. Religion signifies love and respect. This institution is one we respect and it should be called that aptly. It will house our dreams and aspirations."

He then held his hand up with a partly closed fist. Jha and Sanjay raised their fists as well and shouted "Dharam".

Prakash started the construction on the site with a smile. He had inherited Dharam from his father. Today he was making his legacy. This factory was going to represent Prakash's dream and his hopes.

The village people around Vasantgam were cordial people. They were excited about how fast GIDC was growing. Things were changing rapidly around them and it was becoming a major industrial hub so water and electricity were going to be more accessible than before. Jobs were going to be in abundance as well.

On 30 December 1985, the construction in Vasantgam was complete and the machines had finally been shifted. The new year was going to tide in a new beginning for Dharam.

The Life of a Poor Man's Son

For one who has taken birth, death is certain and for one who is dead, birth is certain; therefore you ought not to lament an inevitable solution (2.27).

—Bhagvad Gita

While Dharam was under construction in Vasantgam, Jha and Sanjay had made trips to the village to make arrangements for the labour force to stay. They were also probably in risk of losing 20-30 percent of their workers because of the shift in location so they had to make arrangements for the shortfall as well.

Dharam was constructed as a shed and there was enough space in the firm for both Jha's and Sanjay's operations. The front part of the building protruded out and there was an RCC construction in that part which stretched up to two floors to accommodate a small storage facility and a room which could be used by Prakash or Sanjay to stay in.

Prakash had also erected a small tank just outside the walls of the building so that any person who was passing by could have access to drinking water. This was meant for the villagers and workers alike. It was his way of giving back to the village.

On the 1 January 1986, the workers assembled inside the factory and there was a prayer ceremony to mark the opening in Vasantgam.

Apart from the workers, the villagers showed up as well. Prakash made sure that everyone who came was given some food.

Prakash got up to address his workers and said, "Dharam is not a factory. It is a dream which Mr. Chand and my father thought of and conceived. Now I am sharing that dream with all of you. Today, we embark on a new journey. Today, we promise ourselves that Dharam will not die – not even with my death. The firm will live a long life and continue to bring prosperity to its employees."

The workers shouted loudly – "Long Live Dharam, Long Live Prakash." The workers then started the machines one by one.

Dharam Synthetics Vasantgam was officially in operation.

The factory started and Sanjay and Jha took charge of their respective departments. Prakash by then had a good idea of how to handle operations and two days of travel every week was sufficient for him to check whether things were going as planned. Prakash had learnt a few cardinal rules of production which he believed helped his cause a lot.

After Dharam moved to Vasantgam Prakash grew both in reputation and stature. He had little influence on the twisting department workers who were quite reticent as a group. He didn't bother much since work was fine and that department was profitable. As far as he was concerned, they were Jha's headache.

Life for the workers started on a happy note in Vasantgam. There was a small school nearby where they could send their children and the cost of living was much cheaper than Bombay so they were able to live better with the same salary.

Raju was one of those men. He worked in Sanjay's department. He had a wife, Savitri, and a son, Suraj. They had a simple life and were happy within their limited means.

One day, Raju was talking to Savitri, "Aren't you happy about moving to this village?"

"I don't know. It just seems so different. Will Suraj have the same life here that he did in Bombay?"

"Yeah, this will be better for Suraj. He is our entire life. You think I will do anything which will not improve his life!"

Savitri looked at Suraj who was busy studying. "He will study and become a big man. He will not be like us. He will live our dreams."

Raju hugged Savitri with tears in his eyes and said, "Yes, he will."

On one fateful day, Suraj was riding a bicycle to his school when a truck hit him from behind. In Vasantgam, the roads were not well made so the traffic at Vasantgam wasn't disciplined and there were many heavy vehicles in the area. Passersby rushed him to the nearby hospital.

When Raju was informed about this, he was at work. When he heard this news, he was aghast.

Prakash was in office that day. He ran to Prakash with tears in his eyes. "Sir, my son just had an accident. He was bleeding on the road. Someone took him to the local hospital. Save him, sir."

Prakash immediately arranged for a car to take Raju to the hospital. Raju sat next to him with a blank look on his face. Jha and Sanjay sat in the back in the car which Prakash drove as fast as he could.

As soon as they reached the hospital, Prakash and Raju rushed to the room where Raju had been taken.

Savitri had already reached there and was crying loudly.

She rushed to Raju and shook him. "My whole life is my son. Save my son. Please do something. *Save him!*"

Raju was in shock, seeing his son lying on the bed in front of him. Prakash was stunned to see the building which passed as a hospital. It was not worthy of being called even a clinic. It did not have any kind of infrastructure and there was no doctor available.

Prakash rushed down to find out if there was a bigger hospital nearby. He was informed that the nearest was an hour away in Vapi. He quickly paid off the money needed to shift Suraj to Jha. Jha rushed to get an ambulance ready while Sanjay went up to be with Raju and Savitri.

Jha managed to get an ambulance and ran upstairs to get Suraj. As soon as he reached, he saw people crying loudly outside. Prakash was seated in a corner silently. Raju and his wife were crying on Suraj's bed. Suraj was lying on the bed listless.

Jha went to Prakash and asked him, "What happened?"

After a while, Prakash looked at Jha and said, "He died, Jha. His son died."

Prakash found it difficult to control his tears. He somehow mustered the courage and walked up to Raju who did not know what to do.

Raju hugged Prakash and started crying.

Prakash had been stoic for a while, but when Raju took his shoulder, tears started flowing from his eyes and he found it difficult to control them.

Raju's wife looked at him and said, "Why did you get us here? Why? This place took my Suraj away from me. Why? What do I live for now?"

Her eyes were red with tears. She had just lost her son. Her life's purpose was Suraj and he was no longer with her.

Raju hugged his wife while Prakash leaned against a wall. All he had heard was, "Why did you get us here?" The words looped in his head because he knew a better hospital could have saved Suraj. Better facilities could have saved him. In fact, better roads could have averted the accident altogether. Was he to blame for this?

Meanwhile, Jha realized Prakash wasn't feeling too well. He sat him down and said, "Sir, I'll book a train back to Bombay. You leave. We'll take care of this."

"I'm not going anywhere, Jha."

"Sir, you leave."

Prakash shouted loudly, "I'm not going anywhere, Jha. I killed him. I killed you all by bringing you here."

Jha turned to Sanjay for help. Sanjay looked at his owner and said, "You should go home, sir."

Prakash folded his hands as if he was requesting both of them. "I need to stay for the funeral. Who will take care of that for them? I need to stay…"

After about three hours, there was a sad silence in the hospital room. Tears had dried up and Raju and Savitri were standing there just staring at their son as if he would get up any minute. They shook him again and again but to no avail.

Some of the workers suggested that they should proceed for a funeral in a timely manner. Jha took Raju aside and told him that. Raju had tears in his eyes and said, "But, I want to be with him a while longer. Please don't take him away now. Please." He folded his hands in front of Jha and burst out crying.

Sanjay went up to Jha and said, "Let him be with his son for as long as he can. His child has been taken away from him. Let him weep in front of his son's body for a while. Maybe it will help take some of the pain away."

Jha started talking to Sanjay about what to do. The funeral had to be done by evening otherwise it would be possible only the next morning. They took a call and decided to do it the next day.

Prakash did not want to move from there. The other workers from the factory had also reached. They were all outside the hospital.

Jha looked at Prakash and said, "They can't see a weak owner, sir. They have to see you composed even now. This is not your fault. It could have happened anywhere."

Prakash took a deep breath and walked out of the hospital. He passed by the workers whom Jha told to come back the next day.

"Sanjay, take Prakash sir to the factory guest house. I will take Raju home and take Suraj's body there. I will stay with them till tomorrow morning."

"Okay. Call us if you need anything."

"Nothing. Just try and make all the funeral arrangements for tomorrow morning."

They took off and reached his house. Raju stayed in a small house situated on a small hilltop at Vasantgam. There were many houses nearby.

The next morning the sun shone with all its brilliance but at Raju's house, nothing was noticed. A lot of people had gathered to offer condolences to Raju and Savitri. Suraj's body was lying outside the house wrapped in a white sheet. Savitri sat beside the body caressing the hair on Suraj's head as if she was lulling him to sleep. She was still in shock at the loss of her son. Raju stood by a pillar, silently letting his tears fall.

Prakash went up to Raju and stood there with tears in his eyes. Raju immediately lay down at Prakash's feet and started crying loudly, "Sir, now what will happen to my wife and me? Who do we earn for? We have lost everything we had."

Prakash hugged him and started crying himself.

After a while, he stepped away and told Jha, "Have they made arrangements for the cremation?"

"I had told Sanjay."

Sanjay immediately replied, "Everything is ready. We just need to take the body to the funeral home. I have arranged for everything we need there."

They arranged for a cot and laid Suraj's body on it.

His wife clung to the cot shouting, "Don't take him away. Please don't take him away. It was not his time to go."

Jha asked the other village women to take her inside the house while they took the body for the last rites. As they moved away with the cot on their shoulders, her shrieks echoed throughout the village, calling out for her son.

Raju was holding the cot at one corner and at the other three corners were Prakash, Jha and Uday Shankar Chaubey.

Meanwhile other workers came to the site as soon as they realized that Prakash, Jha and Sanjay were there. They took the cot from them on the way and proceeded to the cremation site. They reached the site and lay Suraj on a pile of wooden logs as per the Hindu custom.

No one can understand what pain a father feels when he is the one who lights the fire of his young son's pyre.

Raju was in tears and his hands shook when he lit fire to his son's dead body.

Prakash stared at the funeral pyre while it was burning. Jha and Sanjay watched him from the corner of their eyes. At the end of it, Jha turned to Sanjay and said, "You take sir to the factory. I'll take care of Raju and his wife and settle all the accounts with the funeral home."

Sanjay nodded his head in okay.

Prakash quietly got into the car and went back to the factory. Jha reached there. Sanjay immediately booked a ticket on the last train back to Bombay. He got some food but Prakash wouldn't touch it.

Meanwhile, Jha came back and said "Sir, please have some food."

He looked at Jha and said, "It's all a waste. We should shut this company down. It's all a waste."

Jha stared at Prakash. "What about the three hundred other children who are being fed because of this firm? Should they be allowed to starve to death because of what happened?"

"What did Raju do to deserve this? Does his son's life have no value? Who does he live for now? How do we compensate him for his loss? His son was all he had, all that he was working for. Nothing we do can bring his son back."

"This could have happened anywhere. It's not your fault. We need to be with Raju and give him a reason to restart his life. You need to go home today and relax, sir. You've been through a lot."

Sanjay took the car to drop Prakash to the station. The moon shone in the night sky surrounded by glittering stars. All the way, Prakash remained silent and stared at the night sky with a blank expression on his face.

He went back to Bombay that day with a heavy heart and mind. It was as if Prakash had lost his own son. The entire trip, Prakash was hounded by one question the answer to which he could not get: "Is Dharam worth the life of a poor man's son?"

Trouble in Paradise

The qualities of goodness, passion and ignorance thus produced by the material energy enslaves the immutable, consciousness of the self within the body (14.5).

—*Bhagvad Gita*

It took Prakash some time but he eventually got over Suraj's death and Dharam continued its operations. It flourished in Vasantgam. There were the occasional problems that they encountered but the company was overall making a decent amount of profit and by God's grace, was never short of demand.

Meanwhile, Prakash was falling in love with the beautiful and sensible Sushma. Sushma was a sweet looking girl who was blessed with really sharp features. She was decently educated and very smart and forward thinking.

Prakash had been meeting up with her earlier and had fallen head over heels in love. Sushma could counter Prakash on every point that he made. Her intellect, humility had brought her very close to Prakash. Their first meeting had been with their families as was the tradition in those days. They were told to spend some time together before they took a final decision.

They took off for a stroll in the park nearby. Both of them were quite shy initially and Prakash was checking her out from the corner of his eye.

He then mustered the courage and asked her, "So, what's your name?"

Sushma laughed and gave him a smile. "Didn't anyone tell you my name before you were going to meet me?"

Prakash was taken aback for a while. "They told me your name's Sushma."

"They were right, actually. You should trust your elders."

Prakash wasn't one to back off so easily, "Oh. They also told me you were fat and ugly. That wasn't true. So, I presumed they were lying about everything."

"Hmm…A smart ass. Is this smartness going to continue if we get married?"

"It might just get worse."

"Great, then what are we waiting for. We have a lifetime of wisecracks to share with each other waiting for us."

"You didn't ask me if I was ready to marry you."

Sushma smiled and took out a small mirror from her purse and pointed it at him. "Now, Seriously, look at this…" and then pointed it towards her while making her hair, "Look at this." She repeated this for three or four times before Prakash finally asked, "What's your point?"

"What? You haven't got it yet. Average looking and average brains. You're the whole package, aren't you? The point, Mr. Prakash, is I'm the best a guy like you is going to get in this lifetime. Next life, if you're born as a Rajesh Khanna or his son's son, you might get better. This life, it doesn't get better than this."

Prakash smiled, "I have money and my own factory."

"That just spoils it even further. You'll end up living your life in the factory. I am ready to marry you despite that."

"Why are you saying yes?"

"You look like someone who I can dominate easily. That's the whole point."

Prakash couldn't help smiling.

Both of them communicated their decision to their respective families and were thereby, engaged to be married on a later date. Even urban Indian families in those days were quite conventional in their thinking so that was actually ahead of their times. Their families, especially Sushma's, were quite forward so the engagement was now their licence to date. Chand was cool with anything and everything that Prakash did. For him, Prakash was his poster boy who could do no wrong.

Prakash and Sushma met many times after that evening.

Jha once caught his boss leaving early from office, "Where are you going, sir?"

Sanjay was nearby and realized it was time to gang up on Prakash. "Yeah sir, where are you going?"

"I have to go early. I have to meet a customer."

"Which customer are you going to meet, sir? Fabric related or yarn related?"

Prakash was getting a bit impatient. He had promised Sushma he would take her out to a nice restaurant in the evening. They had to leave early so that they could get back on time as Sushma had a strict 9:30 p.m. deadline.

"I'm going to meet a fabric related customer."

Sanjay immediately jumped in, "Who, sir?"

Jha retorted, "She's 5'4", fair and he's probably going there to talk about women's wear."

"Women's wear. That's interesting. What is her name, sir?"

"No, no. I'm going to meet a male customer."

Sanjay grinned and Jha was smiling as well. Prakash was blushing like a teenager who had just been confronted about his first love.

"We talk to Chand, sir. We know who she is. We want you to tell us the truth."

"Her name's Sushma..."

Jha immediately shouted, "*Sushma Bhabhi*. What a name? Sir, the name brings music to my ears. We should call her here and tell her all about you."

Prakash almost spoke matter of fact like an innocent child, "She won't marry me then."

Both Sanjay and Jha laughed and after teasing him a little longer, they let Prakash go. He had been taking off early in the recent days and had assumed everything was right with the firm. Jha knew these were his days of yore and he was not willing to spoil them.

Sanjay looked at Jha and said, "Did you tell him?"

Jha shook his head and sighed, "No, I didn't. Don't tell him now."

"We need to. The situation might worsen."

"I know. I just don't want to spoil his mood now. There does not seem to be a quick and easy solution."

"He deserves to know. It's his factory."

"Right. Wish I could buy some time or do something about it myself, though."

"You can't, Jha. You've tried and failed."

Jha shrugged Sanjay off and walked off from there.

Meanwhile, Prakash was in a carefree mood when he went to meet the love of his life. He went to her place to pick her up. It was a clear night with a full moon and the stars clearly visible. She was beautifully dressed in a gown and the moonlight bounced off her.

"You're late."

"Well, two jokers were taking my case back there in the company."

"Jokers?"

"Oh, you have no idea. These are complete idiots."

"Well, they work for you. They have to be idiots."

Prakash contracted his eyes and gave her a sly look. "You watch it there, madam. I can still break it off."

Sushma responded back with a smug grin, "My brothers will break your head."

Prakash shook his head in disagreement, "Yeah right."

"You try it. I dare you to."

Love was in the air for both Prakash and Sushma. It was a special feeling. Prakash needed her in his life. Sushma had become his primary purpose, around whom everything else seemed so secondary. This included his factory.

Prakash returned home that evening feeling very light-hearted when he got a call from Jha.

He said, "I need to talk to you tomorrow morning."

"Is everything okay?"

"Not really."

"What happened?"

"It's about the twisting employees. There are some weird happenings in the company."

"Okay. I'll be there."

Next day, Prakash went to the factory and immediately called Jha. "What happened?"

"Nothing has been going right with twisting. You have not noticed but the production levels are down. The employees have become very rebellious and are objecting to everything from the work to the tea. There is news that some are coming to work drunk and there are even reports of people doing drugs."

"What? Drinks. Drugs. What's going on, Jha? Does Chand know about this?"

"No. He's busy with his work. You take care of production issues."

"Why wasn't I informed earlier?"

"I thought I could take care of it by removing those workers. Apparently, they have been well informed of the labour laws in the country and they threatened me with labour cases when I tried to. They have been educated by the pseudo politicians that roam outside the area about the cruelties that we exert on them and the remedies available to them in case we take any action. One of them is also related to a politico whose assistant called to rebuke and threaten me to be careful with these employees. We aren't doing everything according to the book."

"What are we not doing according to the book?"

"The most important provision that we are not following is the minimum wage. Since they work in a twelve hour shift and the rule book defines eight hour shifts, we are supposed to pay two times the wage of the eight hour shift. That makes everything unviable because you have to change the wages of every employee from the operator to supervisor to technician. There are some other small provisions that we are not following. When you have one big fault, the other small ones open up as well."

"Like you said, the market is also not doing everything according to book."

"Prakash, the market isn't the one caught in this muddle. We are. The labour courts and the politicos outside assume ignorance unless someone reports it."

"So we are basically stuck with rebellious labour."

"Yes."

"How bad is it?"

"Prakash, before Dharam I was working in an organization as a supervisor. It was a good firm and the people were good. I left from there because labour issues went out of control. The entire workforce went rebellious. The company was not allowed to operate because the politicos kept on issuing notices. That was followed up by bribes which needed to be given periodically to keep them at bay and to reach a settlement. Over time, different politicos had different vested interests in the organization. The owner was even arrested. He then somehow settled the dues and shut the firm down. This needs to be controlled now."

Prakash looked at Jha and sighed "We ran away from Bombay because of these problems and here I am staring at them again."

Dharam was in turmoil. This wasn't a minor problem which would go away easily.

The Battle Begins

Either being slain you will attain the heavenly worlds or by gaining victory you will enjoy the earth; therefore O Arjuna confident of success rise up and fight (2.37).

—*Bhagvad Gita*

Prakash wanted to tackle this problem head on. It was the first time he was facing a union problem and he was irritated that there was no immediate solution to it. He was surprised that even in private companies, the labour laws and politicos outside were so strong that his hands were basically tied. He could not fire anyone that easily.

There was a reason that Prakash was not aware of the happenings. He wasn't that focused on the twisting department and trusted Jha. He asked Jha to get the reports immediately. Jha came in with the production reports of the previous three months.

Prakash saw them and asked him "What's our capacity?"

"45 tonnes."

"How much are we doing currently?"

"30 tonnes."

"What? In 30 tonnes, production costs shoot up. Aren't we at a loss?"

"I told you we are not doing well."

Prakash lost his cool and raised his voice at Jha, "You didn't tell me we are doing this badly, Jha. This is ridiculous. You are responsible, Jha. This division was your responsibility."

Jha was a hard-headed Bihari and was not used to being shouted at. He shot back, "It is your fault as well, Prakash. While you have been roaming around with your girlfriend, we have been trying to tackle this problem the as best as we can."

Prakash was stung by the 'girlfriend' comment. He shouted loudly at Jha, "Get lost from this room and from my company."

"Okay, sir. I will do that."

Jha walked out of the room, angry and hurt about what had happened. How dare Prakash talk to him like that? He had been the one who had got Prakash to this level and this was how Prakash was repaying him?

He walked out of the firm in anger. Not very far from the firm, there was a tea shop with some chairs. The chairs were lined under a tarpaulin sheet to keep the sun away. Tired workers would often sit there and beat the heat. Jha sat quietly on a chair, sulking. He had never felt this bad before.

Prakash put his hands on his head and sat down for a while. He cooled down and walked out of his cabin to search for Jha. He found him sulking at the tea shop.

Jha saw Prakash and immediately looked the other way. Prakash asked the shop-owner for two cups of tea."

Jha shook his head and said, "I have had my tea. I don't need you to buy me tea. I have taken enough from you."

Prakash patted Jha on the back. "Let's go to my cabin."

Jha looked at Prakash and smiled. "First, finish your tea. Then let's go in."

After a while, Jha went into Prakash's cabin with him.

Jha gave him a letter. "Here, this is my resignation."

Prakash tore it and said, "Go back to work, Jha."

"You told me to leave the firm."

"Jha, we have bigger things to think about. If you want me to say sorry, I will. Go back and work."

Jha realized his boss was sorry and sat down. "I'm sorry as well for the girlfriend comment. That was out of line."

"That's okay. I have been slightly distracted from work."

"No, no. You've been giving your hours, don't worry. This is a temporary problem, Prakash. We will get over this."

"How do you propose that?"

"Let's try and talk to these workers. I'll call them and you address them about your problems. Maybe, we can gain their sympathy given that we are facing a loss."

"Before we do that, let's see if we can first figure out the wrongs and who is involved in what. There has to be a leader given that they are in a rebellious mood. Have you figured out who the leader is?"

"Not really. It looks like it's either Foudhar or Uday. I knew when I was recruiting Uday, the guy could mean trouble but I recruited him nevertheless."

"Let's find out who is involved in what here. Let's segregate the operators that come to work drunk, the ones are actually doing decent work and ones who are shirking work on paper. We should know what we are up against before we talk to them. How many of them are there?"

"Thirteen."

"If you talk to one of them, the others would get to know. Then it would be open war. It's them against us. We already have a sense of who's with us and who's against us."

"It is already them against us, Jha, at least by what you've told me.

"Yeah, but if you try to split them outright, they come under risk. There is an incentive for the other workers to isolate and pressurize them."

"Who is on our side? You probably know the ones who are sincere to the company and the ones that are not."

"Yeah, I do. Sevak Ram, Om Prakash Yadav, Avdesh Pandey and Kranti Kumar are sincere to the firm."

"Who are the rebels?"

"The rest. Ramraj, Jawahar Lal Shinde, Umesh Yadav, Mohan Singh, Radhe Shyam, Vinay Pandit and P. Vijay Kumar are with Uday and Foudhar."

"We have two groups. That's nine versus four. It seems stacked against us. I'll talk to them and try and see if I can tackle their problems."

"Even if we tackle the production issues, what about the alcohol and drugs?"

"Are these gang leaders Uday and Foudhar the ones who are drinking alcohol?"

"Uday does not drink or smoke. He seems to be a very different man. I doubt if he even cares about the monetary increase. He speaks little but whenever he does, he talks about social injustice and how he is against it."

"So, he isn't basically a bad man then."

"I would not say a bad man, but a stubborn man. He is very difficult to convince and even more difficult to buy off. You can't tempt him with anything. I tried hinting at that and he simply scoffed at me. He's more dangerous than anyone I've met. Some people can't be bought, bargained or negotiated with. They don't care if the world burns and they burn along with it. They want to know if '*justice*' as they know it is served, and Uday is one of those people."

"Well, if we can convince him that we are not wrong, he will be with us. That's what we want. Let's just talk to him and ask him if we're doing anything that displeases him."

"Okay. That seems fine. I'll call him down then."

Jha brought Uday to Prakash's office.

Uday was tall, well-built and had a huge moustache with curls. Prakash was thinking in his head, "My God, we've hired *Gabbar Singh* himself."

Uday stood in front of Prakash, waiting for Prakash to ask a question.

"Uday, is there something that we are doing wrong as a firm which is against the welfare of workers?"

Uday shot back, "Yes."

Prakash was stunned at the quick reply. He paused for a bit and asked him, "What are we doing wrong?"

"Well, we are underpaid according to labour laws and overworked. Minimum wages have been defined according to eight hours of labour. If we work more, we are entitled to overtime. We are exploited at every turn. Even the tea served in the factory is not worthy of drinking. All the workers have not been enrolled for pension and they do not get 45 days of paid leave according to the law."

Prakash tried to explain his side of the story. "The production figures are down. Costs are spiralling up. Competition in this market is growing. We can't afford overtime or three shifts according to the eight hour policy. We will end up being ruined."

"I don't care what others are doing. My concern lies with the company I work for. These are just some of the violations that I have told you, there are many others."

Prakash was slowly losing his cool. "If the company is so bad, why are you still with the firm? Why don't you leave us?"

Uday's eyes went red with rage "Why should I leave? I do my work well. I only ask for justice."

Prakash got argumentative. "What do you mean? We are unjust. Go outside and try working with the other factory owners. You'll realize how easy we have made it for you. You people are not worth it."

Jha realized Prakash was attacking Uday and no good was going to come out of this conversation. He told Uday, "Let's go."

Prakash stopped Jha. Uday seemed unwilling to move.

The conversation heated up further. Uday said, "What do you mean we are not worth it? You are where you are, sir, only because of your birth. We are here because of our destiny. We work hard so that people like you can travel in cars."

"You don't think I work hard?"

"You sit in an office while we toil day in and day out to get production on your machines. We are the ones who burn our hands to make sure you have a comfortable life while we struggle for a daily wage."

"Who are you to judge my work? Who are you to lead my labourers?"

"I am their representative."

"What?"

"Yes."

"Let's check with the operators if you really are their representative." He then looked at Jha, "Call the operators down, Jha."

Jha realized this was a huge mistake so he stopped Prakash, "No, sir. We will deal with this later."

By this time, Prakash's ego and temper were out of control. He shouted at Jha, "Call them down, *now!*"

Jha had no choice. He called his operators down. They came down one by one.

Prakash showed them the production figures, "Have you people seen these?"

One of them, Foudhar, replied, "Yes sir, what is your point?"

"These figures are bad, really really bad. How can you even stand in front of me after these?"

Foudhar shot back, "Sir you are still earning because of the labour we put in."

Prakash, losing his temper, said in a slightly shocked voice, "What? I am earning because of you?"

"Yes, sir. You are using our efforts to make a lot of money and you're giving nothing back to us."

Prakash's voice was gradually increasing, "What money? I am not making money here, I am losing money."

"No sir. You're lying."

Prakash then pointed his finger at Uday, "Has he told you this?"

"He is one of us, sir. We all know this."

Prakash was exasperated, "How dare you tell me I'm lying? You all are worthless. I want you out of my company. Get out... all of you. Please. Get out."

"Why should we leave, sir? You can't just fire us like that."

"I can. It is my company. You understand? *My* company. You don't tell me what to do."

Jha tried to calm Prakash down but he was agitated beyond reason. He looked at Jha and said "These guys are taking me for a ride. These good-for-nothing b★★★★★."

Jha stared at Prakash blankly. He had just abused an already agitated work group. It was a grave error. The workers stayed silent. Prakash sat down with his hands on his head. Jha gave him a glass of water and told the workers to go away and leave him in peace.

The workers quietly left. They had got what they wanted. Prakash had abused them and Jha sighed. Prakash had committed a rash mistake. The workers had just gained the upper hand in a struggle that was now very much out in the open.

The battle between Prakash and Uday Shankar Chaubey had just begun.

It Happens this Way Only

O Arjuna, the discrimination of even the knowledgeable is covered by this perpetual enemy in the form of lust, which is like an insatiable fire (3.39).

—Bhagvad Gita

Prakash realized his mistake when he went home. He knew he could not take it back. He could not apologize because that would mean admitting the mistake that he had just committed. He wished he could take it back as his ego had got the better of him at that instant and he had unnecessarily reacted harshly.

Prakash hoped against hope that it was over. He wished that he had one more chance to talk to those workers before they did anything drastic. It was wishful thinking because the group was waiting for a trigger and Prakash had blasted a bomb.

As expected, the workers were outside Dharam on a strike when Prakash came to the factory the next day. The twisting section was on strike because their owner had abused them. It was beneath their rights and dignity to work now. They were not able to stop the company from operating because the other workers pretty much didn't care about what was going on.

Jha was on the gates talking to one of them. Prakash went in the firm and called Jha, "What's going on?"

"They don't think that it's fair their owner thinks that they don't know the name of their parents."

"What?"

"Well, you called them b*****."

"Jha, stop being a joker. What do they want?"

"They want you to apologize."

"That's okay. I need to apologize anyway. I've been feeling bad ever since I used that word on them."

"You call me that every day. You owe me a thousand apologies."

"Well, you deserve to be called that. Call them in."

"Okay."

Jha called them in one by one and Prakash apologized to each one of them. "I'm sorry if I've hurt your feelings. I did not mean to be abusive. I apologize and I hope that you can forgive me, and continue working in the best interest of the firm."

He said this thirteen times without changing the discourse much. It seemed to him like the employees took it well. His thirteenth apology was to Uday who just stood still and blankly stared at him. Jha looked at him and sighed. Uday had been his biggest error in judgement.

They went out and Prakash said, "I just used an abusive word once. I've heard so many industry owners use the term. You should tighten the screws on the employees. They routinely abuse. I abused them once and ended up apologizing."

"Prakash, the environment in our case was already agitated. We ended up making things worse when you abused them. It was a mistake. People tighten the screws on supervisors, not on workers. Supervisors can abuse workers. Owners sometimes get away with a lot of things. An owner I worked with threw a slipper at a worker. He got away with it because no one raised his voice. But, these are workers who have been clearly educated by a politico, Prakash. You knew that. They were already on the edge and you pushed them over."

"Yeah. I know. You think this is over?"

"I don't know. I hope this incident is over."

"I would hope so too. At least, this abuse thing should go away."

Prakash started to focus on other things and forgot about it. Jha went back to work. He was worried about one thing. The employees had gone away and had not reported to work. There were two possibilities – one was that they knew that they were going to be paid for that day anyway so they didn't need to work. The other one was that they were hatching something against the firm. He prayed to God that it wasn't the latter.

Sanjay had a strong grip on those workers and he knew how to extract the maximum from them. Chand was doing well on the marketing front and was extracting decent margins. The fabric division was doing really well too.

Prakash called Sanjay in for a conversation. "The production report seems okay."

"Yeah, we're fine. In fact, your decision to up the speeds of the machines helped us push the production capacities and even though our efficiencies are the same, our production levels are sky high."

"Right. So, our overheads are down?"

"Yeah."

"Jha should be told the fabric division is making much more profits than yarn."

Prakash smiled. "Sometimes, I wonder if you two work for improving the company's future or just showing off that one is better than the other."

"Obviously we work for the company's future here and no offence but there is no competition between me and Jha. I am a much bigger asset to the firm. He knows that."

Prakash gave a tired smile. "Yeah. I'm sure."

Sanjay sensed a bit of tension on his owner's face. "Are you tense about the thing with the workers in the twisting department?"

"Yes."

"Don't worry. Things will get sorted out."

•

"Will they? I'm worried workers in your department will also get affected."

"You're thinking too much. We're doing really well in the fabric department and it is because of your decisions. I did not believe we would end up where we are when it started out with you. The workers there respect you as if you are some God."

"Their feelings are not shared by the workers in twisting. They might influence your workers as well. Do you think I should keep a manager here and focus on sales?"

"Chand is doing sales. You are good at production. A manager would spoil things. Every firm that has been destroyed by union problems has been either because the owners themselves wanted to sell their land and get rid of the industry that they are in, or because some manager had a large ego and wanted the workers to listen to him and got too aggressive with them. Owners who want to run their firms at any cost like you don't mind sacrificing their egos, but managers don't care. It's not their money."

"I so want to get rid of those workers. The twisting department is just a waste of our time and money."

"Yeah. But I don't think you can do that easily."

"No. I've got a whole team that's led by their leader Uday Shankar Chaubey against me now. He won't let me fire anyone."

Meanwhile, Prakash got a call on his factory landline number. He started talking in a softer tone and Sanjay immediately knew who was on the other line. He gave Prakash a teasing smile and left the room."

The voice on the other end of the line was soft and soothing. "Are you okay?"

"Yes. I guess so."

Sushma knew Prakash well. She sensed that Prakash was tense. "Well, you sound tense."

"I'm facing labour problems in my factory."

"Oh. So, are they very serious?"

"Yeah"

"Right. Have you had your lunch?"

Prakash smiled and said, "No. It feels good that there's someone who cares whether I've had my lunch or not."

"There is and there always will be. You are going to marry me, right?"

"As of now, yes."

"You will face much deeper problems if you back out, Prakash."

"Yeah, I'm thinking it might be easier to negotiate with the labourers than with you."

"You bet. You might get some concessions with the workers but you'll never get any with me,"

"Yeah."

Prakash sighed and became pensive. Sushma sensed it and said, "Hey, don't worry. You are a nice man. Good things happen to nice people like you."

Prakash smiled and was about to keep the phone down when Sushma suddenly said, "Take care."

Prakash garnered some strength in his voice. "Yeah, yeah. You don't worry."

He kept the phone down and was lost in thought when Jha suddenly walked in with a paper in his hand. "There's been a problem."

"What?"

"We have a labour court summons."

Prakash's eyes widened with surprise, "What are they summoning us for?"

"A lot of things. Apparently, we've violated multiple labour laws. We are supposed to operate only for eight hours. If we operate for twelve, we are supposed to pay overtime. There are other violations as well. Oh, and wait, here is the kicker. There are allegations of cruelty against you and the fact that you abused these workers."

Prakash took the notice from Jha's hand and gave Jha an exasperated expression. "What do we do now?"

"We wait for the hearing."

"What about the workers in the meantime?"

"It is pretty much up to them now whether they choose to work or not. We have no say in the matter from here on. The ball is in their court."

"Jha, this seems like a no-win situation. We're trapped."

"There is one solution. We need to find out the particular labour court judge who will handle our situation and approach him. We need to buy his support."

"We have to bribe him?"

"Yeah, there is no other choice. Even after you bribe him, Prakash, he will give the workers some compensation to save some face in front of workers, but it might not be that bad."

"Right. If there is no other alternative, let's pay him off. Let's get rid of the menace once and for all by taking his help."

"To get rid of all these employees in one shot is going to be difficult."

Prakash was panicky. "Jha, this situation is getting worse by the day. We need a way out."

"Right."

The images of the labour unrest in his last firm flashed in his head. The long protests, the endless negotiations and the dharnas finally caused the firm to shut down. Jha silently thought to himself, "I hope this company doesn't go through the same inferno that my last company did."

Injure When Injured

What incites one to commit sinful acts is lust, arising from the mode of passion; know this lust to be insatiable, extremely sinful and the greatest enemy in this world (3.37).

—Bhagvad Gita

The labour court judge was a fat guy called Joshi. He was round-faced, stocky and almost always had gutkha in his mouth and would spit it around the village leaving his mark everywhere. He had a huge moustache which served him well in the village because it gave him an intimidating look. He was very 'comfortable' in his government job and hardly worked. He mocked and represented a legislative system that had failed in its entirety in the country.

Joshi was very reclusive and it was proving very difficult to contact him. Jha knew it was important to talk to him before the hearing which was scheduled in a week's time. He scouted around people he knew in the area to find out if there was a way to get in touch with him.

Jha approached a man named Patel who was close to Joshi and asked him if he could have a few words with him. Patel was a short, stocky, bald guy who was popularly known as Joshi's agent. Joshi was a very smart man. He had a foolproof system to collect bribes. He never took them directly lest someone was watching. If someone approached him bluntly offering a bribe, he threatened to put the concerned party in jail. How dare someone assume he was corrupt? He decided what each case that Joshi and the other lawyers in the labour court decided on were worth.

Patel saw Jha and immediately said, "I thought you would come."

Jha smiled. "You know why I've come?"

"Whenever Joshi signs a notice, I find out everything about the company he's sent a notice to. We find out the company's worth, how much they make, who are the major employees, etc. We also know the company's representative who is going to approach us."

"So that you know how much you can take them for."

"You're smart. You've figured it all out. We're like bankers who need to know your value to determine how much we should charge you."

"Yes. You're exactly like bankers. So let's cut to the chase. How much is it going to cost us?"

"You seem in a hurry. Let's go to that tea stall and we can discuss about this over tea."

Jha knew that it was important to please Patel. He walked over to the tea stall and sat down with Patel, even though his slick manner was really putting him off.

When the cups of tea were placed in front of them, Jha asked again, "So how much is it going to cost us?"

"Rupees one lakh," said Patel very coolly.

"What? One lakh is too big an amount."

"Look. The workers are demanding overtime for the last five years that they have been working with you here. You realize how much that is? For the thirteen workers alone the damages could be five to seven lakhs. That is not all. He also needs to pay them at least ten thousand each so the net is going to be two-and-a-half lakhs."

"So that you can show you sided with them as well."

"You're very sharp, you know. Ever thought about becoming a labour court judge?"

"No. Clearly it is very profitable."

"Yes. Joshi takes two international vacations every year, you know. He has a lot of cash expenses. Recently, he bought a five thousand-rupee watch. It's expensive to be a labour court judge, you know. There's so much competition between labour court judges of different jurisdictions."

"Yes, yes. I can understand completely."

"He's now targeting to buy a car, you know. There is now a new model of Maruti, Zen, which is very popular among these judges."

"Right. Dharam would be the first down payment of the Zen."

Patel smirked. "You are very smart. You don't even need an LLB to be an agent. Seriously, do you want me to refer you to any of these other judges? A lot of good money."

"No thanks."

"You know what, I like you. I will talk to Joshi about considering a concession."

Jha was feeling irritated with the conversation. He had half a mind to tell Patel to go to hell with his job offer which had according to him ill-earned money that could lead to no good. But, he knew his position was compromised with him. Patel was the only route to Joshi and Uday and team were after Prakash's case. They needed to make sure all the external elements who could play a role in this *battle royale* were on Prakash's side if Dharam had to survive.

Jha immediately told him, "I'll talk to my boss about this. Meanwhile, you tell him we are going to come up with an answer soon."

"Come back real soon."

"Yeah."

"He has to pay for the Zen really fast. Why do you think he scheduled your hearing so early?"

Jha looked at him and smiled. As he was about to get up Patel remarked, "Thank you for the tea." Jha opened his wallet and took out some change to pay for the tea, taking the hint from the remark.

He then turned his back to him, disgusted at the open nature of corruption at play in the state machinery and the cheapness that the judges and their agents displayed.

He went back to Prakash who was eagerly waiting for him to come back. As soon as he reached, Prakash called him to his cabin.

"What did he say?"

"He's asked for a lakh. Do you want to pay that?"

"What do we get? Will these guys then stop pestering me?"

"Well, it's just not that. He's saying that there would be a lakh and fifty thousand rupees as additional expenditure on the workers' compensation. He says based on the number of stipulated hours per shift, we have overtime of at least four hours over five years every day for thirteen workers. That comes to a claim of five to seven lakhs."

"What? Are you joking?"

"No. That's what he said."

Prakash sighed. "Man, what crap have we gotten into? Can you get it down?"

"Probably can get the entire amount shaved off to two lakhs. Not below that."

"Okay. Try and get it down. Re-negotiate as much as possible. Can we get rid of these thirteen guys after that?"

"Not immediately. Every viral infection takes time to cure, sir. We'll have to find strong reasons and take them out one by one."

"Is there a registered union at this place?"

"There is one. They haven't approached it yet. The worry is..."

"What? What do we have to worry about that's worse than this?"

"They have multiple options outside."

"Do they?"

"Yeah, they do. They can go from one door to another. You can only be on the defensive here."

"We are not a socialist economy, are we?"

"May I say something, sir?"

"Yes."

"These laws are not bad. If you look at a worker's life, you won't be happy. You cannot imagine living their life, sir. They struggle to survive every day. Their wives and kids constantly try to manage within their means. You see an industrialist's kids or even white collar employees and their kids. They cry and get what they want. When they throw a tantrum, it is mostly because they didn't get that toy or that expensive item. When a worker's child cries, it is because he hasn't been fed."

Prakash interrupted him, "We are at the outset a welfare country, aren't we?"

Jha continued his discourse, "We are not a welfare country. We are very much a country which gives the rich what it wants. These laws come into play for votes and for power play only. If they are used well, they can give the worker what he deserves – a decent life."

"But Jha, the whole market has to follow these regulations if it has to work. Otherwise our costing will not be competitive at all."

Jha sighed. "I know that but it sometimes seems that we are not right. These groups deserve more. The system is not strong enough to get them what they deserve."

Prakash intervened, "Jha, we give them much more than the market already. We give them rent, pay them double on holidays if they show up. The only time I've mistreated them is when I let my ego get the better of me and I abused them. These guys are unyielding. Everything we do is wrong for them."

Jha took a deep breath. He appeared partially convinced and said, "Don't worry. We will get rid of these workers in due time."

Jha started to get up to leave. While leaving he smiled and told Prakash, "By the way, that Joshi offered me a job."

Prakash smiled. "Are you taking it?"

"No! These people, Prakash, will suffer one day. There will be karma in this life or the next."

"I guess so."

"Meanwhile, in this life, he's getting a brand new Zen."

"What?"

"Forget it. I'll handle this."

Prakash had apprised Chand of the situation but Chand had no clue of labour laws so he told Prakash to handle it in the best way he could. Prakash got a book on labour laws and started studying the subject. It was very alien to him – sections, subsections, case laws et al. But, he had realized you've got to know the law to fight against it or to defend yourself against it.

Jha spent the next two days meeting Patel. Patel's bribery agency was quite popular among many companies in GIDC. They searched for issues to give notices to firms. More and more companies were coming to the village so Patel and Joshi were doing really well. Joshi was the least liked and had zero knowledge about anything. So he was sent to this village.

As luck would have it, after the 1983 strike, industries started to move there. It became a goldmine for Joshi. Apparently, a small politico related to one of the thirteen guys had alerted them of a certain situation. He had instigated Uday and company about the wrongs done to them.

Simultaneously, he apprised Patel of the situation and took his fees for that. Patel met up with Uday and empathized with him. He convinced Uday to send him a notice.

Patel took Jha to Joshi so that the final negotiation could be closed with him. They went to the labour court office which was in a very dilapidated condition. Every year, money was taken for the repairs of that office which was eventually spent on improving Joshi's personal residence. There was a chair and a table. The chair was rickety and the table was dirty and worn out. The walls had developed cracks and the paint had started to peel off.

Joshi was a fat bloke with a weird Bhojpuri accent and a stinking mouth as if all the evil of the world had accumulated there. He was wearing an unkempt shirt, slightly torn trousers and spectacles. His slippers were outside his office and he was by far the worst excuse for a judge anyone could imagine.

Joshi looked at him with a wicked smile. His prey was here. "Have a seat, Jha."

"You know my name."

"You are from Bihar, no?"

"Yes."

"I am also from Bihar. You know, they say every house in Bihar produces a criminal, a politician and a bureaucrat. It is in our blood to deal with politics. I am a combination. A perfect combo deal."

Jha smiled. "Yes, sir. I have heard a lot about you."

"Good things, I hope."

"Oh yes. Very good things."

"Now you're lying. I've never done anything good so why will you hear good things?"

"You pretend to do good."

"Ahaa, Patel you're fired. I like this man. You want to be my agent?"

Patel looked at Jha and then at Joshi, "He has a lot to learn."

Jha sighed. "Sir, what about our case?"

"You have to pay them ten lakhs."

"What?"

"Yes. I am a good man, Jha. I don't listen to anything wrong. I have expensive habits but I am a very good man."

"Yes, sir."

"These habits are also very costly."

"Yes, sir."

"That Uday is a gem of a worker. He came directly to my office as if he owned it. I told him to calm down and told him that he will get justice."

"Right."

"By the way, do you guys do any background check? Apparently, he's been fired from three companies for his constant want of justice. He's also maimed his father and grandmother in the past."

Jha's face changed but he did not let the shock show too much. "What?"

"Yes, he can't be bought, negotiated or bargained with. Some people are worthless."

"Right."

"I can be bought, you know. My rate had been indicated to you by Patel, I believe."

"Right."

He banged the gavel hard on the table and it almost broke. "One lakh for me it is. Next case, Patel."

"Sir, please bring it down."

"Patel, tell him this is not a fruit shop. I hate ladies because they bargain for just a rupee."

"Sir, please. We are a small setup."

"Your company has a net turnover of Rs 5 crores and a profit of Rs 35 lakhs and this is stated profit. The black earnings must be double of these."

Jha stared at him. He was not aware of these figures himself. "Sir, please, sir. Most of the profit is in stock and with debtors. We have very little cash. You are God, sir."

Joshi liked the God statement a lot. "You're right, you know. I am God. I decide on people's futures. Companies come and beg. I want you to beg me to reduce the amount."

Jha swallowed his pride and said without hesitation, "I beg you to reduce the amount."

"Beggars, all of you. You know I failed my final semester in my law course and had to repeat a year but somehow landed a government job. I paid a bribe to get it. It is so difficult to study. Especially labour law is so tough. I failed that exam twice. Yet, here I am. Top rankers now earn less than me and they even pay taxes. There are no taxes on bribes."

"Right, sir. No taxes on bribes. Please, sir. I request you to reconsider the amount."

"75,000 it is. Now get out before I double it."

Jha said, "Sir, the compensation?"

"1.5 lakhs."

"Sir, I beg you again."

Joshi laughed, "1.25 lakhs. You are a good beggar. You cannot be an agent. Now get out."

Jha sighed. "Okay."

Jha went to Prakash and said "It's down to two lakhs."

"Right."

"What happened?"

"I was thinking about what you said. They will keep on going from one place to another."

"Yes. Let's tackle one problem at a time. Let's at least get this judge on our side. Prakash, there is also someone else behind this."

"Who?"

"I don't know but someone is educating these guys. Patel almost revealed his name but stopped midway as if the cat caught his tongue. We need to know who that guy is otherwise this process will not end."

"Okay. For that, we need a guy on the inside."

"Prakash, at this moment no one will openly oppose them. The others will beat the rebel black and blue. For them, this group means unity. Any person who leaves is a threat. You can get lucky and still find that weak link. We have a hint about the people who are not completely against us but we don't know if any of them have any guts to vouch for us."

"So we're stranded. Are we going to get out of this?"

"We have to be strong and calculative. You cannot be compassionate in this process."

Prakash said with a hint of frustration in his voice. "What have we got ourselves into? Maybe we should shut down the firm."

"Prakash, this firm is called Dharam. You know what the *Bhagvad Gita* says about Dharam? *It is better to strive in one's own dharma than to succeed in the dharma of another. Nothing is ever lost in following one's own dharma*. Prakash, this is your Dharam, your life."

Prakash smiled and asked, "By the way, how do you know the *Bhagvad Gita* so well?"

Jha smiled and placed his hands in perfect position so that looked as if he was playing the flute, "Jha. Mahashankar Jha."

The Hearing

The demoniac who are excessively greedy take on huge undertakings to increase their power (16.11).

—Bhagvad Gita

Savitri rebuked Uday. "Clean yourself up. I am not letting you go out like this."

She was the only one Uday listened to. He had promised himself that he would not be like his father. Savitri was sweet, very stable and had a lot of endurance. She had been with Uday through a lot. His fights with supervisors over the years, his abrupt resignations and his constant insistence to get things done his way had taken them through a lot.

She endured everything and the respect that Uday had for her was immense. For a lot of Uday's friends, their wives were bodies meant to be used for pleasure since they could not afford cheaper means of passing time. Uday, however, respected his wife and made sure she was taken care of. He did double shifts and worked very hard so that money was never a problem in the house.

They had married in the village that Uday came from. There was hardly anyone who attended the wedding. It was basically the couple, Uday's mother and Savitri's parents. Uday's mother looked at the couple during the entire function with tear-filled eyes. She couldn't help but look back at everything that both of them had been through.

Four years after his marriage, his mother passed away. Savitri had never seen Uday break down like he did the day his mother died. For

Uday's mother, he was above everyone else. If you had only one person who was your entire life, you would give every ounce of love that you had to that person. When her time was up, the last action that Savitri remembered was her pointing at Uday's photo.

Uday was outside at the time and her death was so sudden he did not get to say goodbye. When he came home, his wife met him outside the door and quietly informed him about his mother's death. He stayed stoic for a while staring at her lifeless body. He did that for a couple of hours with his wife by his side.

The moment when a loved one departs is the worst possible one. Life can, for that brief moment, not get any worse. Uday had dreaded this moment from the day he realized what death was. His worst fear was lying down in front of him bereft of any breath and he was powerless to do anything about it.

He looked at his wife and said, "She had seen nothing but sadness."

His wife hugged him and said, "That's not true, Uday. You've given her many happy moments."

He took her with the help of a few neighbours to the funeral home and performed the last rites. He stood in front of her burning pyre for hours and stared at the pyre. When the last flame had doused, he was taken home by Savitri. His eyes were red and his body was sweating profusely.

After his mother's death, Savitri was all Uday had. He respected her opinion and her wishes. He stayed hungry but made sure Savitri had food. He was careful to not make any noise when she was sleeping and would stare at her silently while caressing her head gently.

Savitri once asked him, "Why are you so angry with the people out there?"

"They are not fair. God has not been fair with me."

"Are you not happy living with me?"

"I am very happy with you but it depresses my heart that I can't give you a better life because of who I am."

"You make sure we're well fed. You give us the best life I could have got."

"Why do rich people have a better life? Why didn't I get an opportunity to study like them? I could have been better than them at what they do, you know."

"It is destiny. The more you fight it, the more you lose. The more you accept it, the more you will move past it and life might throw you a few opportunities here and there."

He hugged Savitri. His eyes were a bit moist when he said, "He hit her, you know. She didn't do anything wrong. It was not her fault. It was never her fault."

Savitri hugged him back and was in tears. "It was not your fault your father was a horrible man. It is also not anyone else's fault. You don't have to go against the world for that."

"I will not yield. I promised her that I won't. I will not tolerate any sort of injustice done to me or anyone else."

The hearing was due in two days. Prakash was supposed to go to the hearing since his testimony was critical. He was supposed to justify as to why the company worked like it did, going against the labour laws of work hours, minimum wages and workplace conditions. He was also to apologize publicly to the workers for abusing them.

Jha accompanied Prakash to the labour court. He had been careful as to give Joshi only fifty percent of the promised amount. He had told him that the rest would be given only after Joshi resolved the issue completely.

Joshi was late to the court, as usual. So the workers, Prakash and Jha waited outside the court in the heat for a couple of hours beyond the scheduled time.

When he finally arrived, he was a bit drunk. Apparently, an old friend of his met him in the morning and they decided to go for drinks.

He came in and barked at the people outside. "What the hell are you guys doing here?"

"We're here for our hearing."

He stared at Patel. "Is there a hearing?"

Patel stared back. "Yes. There is. But they can come tomorrow if you want."

Joshi immediately barked, "They are dismissed for today then. All of them."

Two hours after waiting in the sun, all of them went back to the company. They took off, disappointed that there had been no resolution that day and irritated with the fact that they had to go again the next day.

The next day, they lined up outside the court again – Prakash, Jha and the employees. It was like going to the principal's office. You stand outside the office waiting for the principal to come, knowing that you will be reprimanded once he or she comes. In this case, the students hoped that the principal wouldn't come to school drunk.

Joshi came in partly drunk. He was sober by his standards so he decided to get on with the hearing. He called them in. Patel came to assist with the hearing and there was an excuse for a legal writer there taking notes.

The proceedings began and Joshi asked Uday Shankar Chaubey, the representative of the workers to present his case first.

Uday started, "Sir, we are employees of Dharam. The company has not been fair to us since we have joined it."

Joshi intervened, "You b★★★★★. What did you want the company to do? Give you a car and a house."

Uday was stunned for a moment, taken aback, by Joshi's response. Jha and Prakash realized it was the bribe and the alcohol talking. Joshi had put the workers on the backfoot and the hearing had not even started yet.

Uday backed up a little. He looked at the other workers who were already scared that things would not go their way.

Uday continued, "No, sir. We don't want that. We have been denied our rights. The minimum wage..."

"Are you a lawyer?"

"No, sir."

"Have you read the law?"

"No, sir."

"Then what the hell do you know about it?"

Uday's temper was gradually increasing. He managed to control it somehow because he knew everything was at stake. If he lost his temper, he would not only be thrown out of the court, but the case would be effectively over.

He stared at the judge for a while and continued, "Our rights including minimum wage and hours per shift have been violated. Conditions of work are not good. We deserve more money, respect and better conditions of work."

Joshi let him complete this time and then looked at the others, "Do you share this view?"

He then turned to Prakash, "What do you have to say?"

"Sir, we try to do the best that we can for the workers. We also have to keep in mind what the other companies are doing."

Joshi interrupted him, "What the other companies are doing is not relevant here."

"It might not be relevant, but truth is we won't survive in the market if they follow one standard and we do the other. Our costing will shoot up and no one will purchase goods from us."

Joshi nodded his head to show some understanding. He then turned to Uday and shouted at him, "Who do you think you are? Datta Samant? You are not a union leader. I will not have unions disturbing industry in this village. These industries lead to jobs. You uneducated people will never understand their importance."

Uday then spoke, "Sir, but that does not mean that they are allowed to wrong us."

Joshi lost his patience and started abusing Uday. "You idiot, good-for-nothing useless b****. You will not speak out of turn."

Uday had half a mind to smash the living hell out of Joshi there and then, but he resisted. Joshi was a powerful man in a high position.

Joshi continued to abuse Uday. Uday shut up and listened quietly. His blood was boiling but he had no outlet for his rage at that moment.

Joshi then looked at the workers and realized he had to balance it a little.

He then turned to Prakash, "You have not been fair to these workers."

Prakash realized there was no point arguing, "Yes, sir. I promise we will make everything right from here on."

"Right, but you must also compensate them for the past."

"Yes, sir."

"Pay them four thousand per worker."

Uday raised his voice to object, "That's not enough, sir."

Joshi now looked at him menacingly. "You are a leader, no? I will put you behind bars if you don't know who you're talking to and shut the hell up."

Uday quieted down and realized he had no say in the matter.

"Okay. We side with the workers more than the owners. Prakash, pay them five thousand rupees each as compensation. Matter closed.'

He banged the gavel on the table to indicate closure. "Now, get lost. All of you."

They walked out of there. For Jha and Prakash, things had gone exactly as they had anticipated. Uday and company realized that they had been short changed.

The first hearing had just concluded similar to many other hearings in the country. It was bought off. It wasn't a fair conclusion and Prakash knew it. He had made up his mind to double the compensation and close this matter. As long as running costs remained the same, he was okay with giving the workers a fair amount.

Uday, meanwhile, was fuming. Nothing about the situation seemed fair to him. He had been humiliated, degraded and justice hadn't been served.

Prakash was hoping the situation had come to an end. In Uday's mind, it was far from over.

Uday went home that day, dejected and disappointed. Savitri served him his dinner and asked him what had happened.

"The judge gave an unfair ruling."

"It's okay, Uday. Our life is okay the way it is."

Uday immediately raised his voice and threw his dinner away. "No, it's not okay. Nothing about life is fair. There is no justice in this world. We reek of the shit that is thrown on us daily by these rich goons. Our sweat and blood mean nothing to them and we are just a small part of their desire to acquire as much wealth as they can at our cost. We churn the wheel while they sit on their chariots. We burn while they switch on their air conditioners. We fear where our next meal will come from while they fulfil their desire for cars and jewels. We are born to be in hell but create a heaven for them to enjoy."

It was the first time Uday had shouted at Savitri after his mother's death. She just stood there, shivering and praying for her husband.

It Ain't Over Yet

Compassion, modesty, gentleness and determination are qualities in one born of divine nature (16.2).

—Bhagvad Gita

It takes time for incidents to be forgotten. The hearing had been just one such incident that had taken place but it had been a valuable learning experience for Prakash. He now had hopes for bringing about changes in the way he ran the company so that he could do more for the workers.

A change was also imminent in his personal life. He was to tie the knot with Sushma. They had been engaged for a year but because of a death in Sushma's house, the wedding had been postponed.

Prakash's love for Sushma grew as time had passed. She calmed him down when he was angry and there had been many such moments in the recent past. He had broken down a couple of times at the hopelessness of the situation with Uday. Sushma brought an element of stability in his life. He could call her and talk about anything and everything.

As was the tradition, the elders decided on an auspicious date for the wedding which was set for the month after the one that Joshi had announced his decision. Her parents were quite open-minded in their thinking so they let her go out with him. They were also scared that Prakash would back off given that the engagement had prolonged for so long. Prakash took complete advantage of their fear and open-mindedness and spent as much time with Sushma as he could.

The park was quite close to Sushma's house. It was lush green and there was a neat walkway in the middle. It was quite large according to Bombay standards and was usually empty on weekends. There were large trees all around, ensuring a decent breeze almost all the time. The grass was mowed and the park was pretty well maintained. There was a corner for kids with a slide and a swing. At the centre of the park, there was a statue. Apparently, it belonged to some politico who had contributed money for the construction of the park.

Prakash was dressed in his office clothes. Sushma was wearing an Indian suit and was looking very pretty. She had minimal make up and was wearing some sort of a cherry lip stick that made her lips look luscious.

Prakash looked at Sushma and said, "Today is a good day."

"Why?"

"Finally, the labour court mess is cleared."

"Yeah. So, is it over?"

"I don't know. I'm hoping and praying to God that it is. We have to still give the workers their compensation. So, we're hoping they don't strike again and accept the deal."

"Well, they will. Even if they don't, I'm sure you'll handle it."

"Yeah. I guess so. By the way, you look beautiful today."

"I do. You don't look that bad either."

Prakash suddenly stopped. He gave her an intense look, "You know I love you a lot."

Sushma gave him a coy smile. "I know you do, sweetheart. I have you whipped."

There was no one in the park that day. It was quite deserted. They walked into a corner. Suddenly, Prakash held her close. They were breathing on each other. Sushma was taken aback at the sudden move, but she didn't resist much. He then brought her lips closer to his and kissed her. They stood lip locked for a couple of minutes before Sushma drew away and playfully punched Prakash on the stomach.

"Can't you wait until we get married?"

"Well, I couldn't resist, you know. Your lips were looking so inviting."

"You are a naughty man. You are not getting anything before our marriage now. I want this trailer to last right up to our wedding day."

Prakash sighed. "Yeah. Just my luck."

They completed the walk without any further incident. Prakash made a few moves but Sushma kept a distance from Prakash and threatened to hit him if he made any move.

For a few hours, Prakash forgot what he had gone through and the risks of the situation continuing the way it was.

The next day when Prakash went to the factory, the twisting workers were working.

He called Jha in. "How is everything? Are the workers okay with us now?"

"No, the situation is not good."

"What do you mean?"

"I tried paying these guys the compensation that Joshi awarded. They did not take it. They said it was too less."

"You should have said it was Joshi's decision to award the payoff. We were not involved in that decision."

"Right. The problem is that they don't care. For them, if they take the payoff, their issues will be deemed settled. They have been instructed not to take it."

"By whom?"

"By that politico type guy apparently. I have tried to talk to one of the guys involved. Sevak Ram. Apparently, Uday learns from that politico and teaches the other workers. He never mentions his name, though."

"We need to find out who he is and try and influence him."

"The problem is that only Uday knows who he is. This guy is well-trained in labour laws and he is filling Uday's head with animosity. Uday already thinks that every rich capitalist is a thief. The more he learns about labour laws, the more he thinks that he is being exploited."

"Yeah, well. What do we do now?"

"We wait. We will pay off Joshi so that he is on our side. That takes one peg off the system."

"Who else do you think they can approach?"

"The local MLA, union leader and the MLA from the opposition are all potential trouble makers. They have many windows still open to them. I guess, till something does not come from their side, it is difficult for us to do anything but to continue as is."

"Can we not start firing them?"

"No. Every worker in your firm knows about these thirteen rebels. So far they are on your side and they think you are in the right. But if you start firing people, they might get it into their heads that you do whatever you want as the owner of the firm. That might prompt the workers you remove to approach as many 'influential' people as possible to defend their interests. They will have a further cause of action against us."

"There are a lot of people who are willing to benefit from this tiff."

"Clearly a whole lot of them have already started getting involved."

"We have everything to lose in this battle. It is not even worth fighting."

"Yes, it is worth fighting to survive. Dharam is our dream, right?"

Prakash looked at him and in a pensive tone and said, "We have nothing going for us, Jha. We have no one on our side."

Jha emphatically opened his shirt displaying his vest and said, "We have. I have my mother."

Prakash looked at him, slightly clenched his teeth and gave him a sly look. "You are joking."

"No, I am not."

"Well, you either have a mother or you deceived me and took a leave and Rs 10,000 advance two years back when you said she died."

"Right. I don't have a mother..." He then looked at Prakash and laughed. "Don't worry. It will all be over soon."

"You think that."

"Yeah, I do."

Jha left the room and Prakash got back to his usual job of looking at his production reports.

The next morning, Prakash got ready to go to work. He took off for the factory. As soon as he reached, Jha was waiting for him.

Jha threw a copy of the local Hindi newspaper down in front of him. Prakash took it from the table. His face went pale as he sat down on his chair.

Politics is a Dirty Game

Possessed of self-conceit, power, insolence, lust and anger the demoniac are always envious (16.18).

—Bhagvad Gita

"LOCAL COMPANY FOUND VIOLATING WORKER RIGHTS. MR. YADAV TO TAKE ACTION AGAINST ERRANT COMPANY"

Last evening, a group of workers working in a local company approached Mr. Yadav with their problems. Their owner, Prakash, has not only violated the basic labour laws of our country but also abused these workers who have put in their blood and sweat for the company. Uday Shankar Chaubey who was the representative of these thirteen individuals approached the local MLA with his problems and hoped that he would get a reasonable solution for their troubles. Mr. Yadav has promised them that they will take action against Dharam and the company will not be allowed to function unless the needs and demands of these workers are met. According to Uday Shankar Chaubey who is leading this struggle against the errant company, they had approached the local tribunal but the judge was biased, most probably because he had been paid off. "Till when will we tolerate this sort of bad governance in our factories? Are we slave drivers or in the true sense, inclusive?" The owners of Dharam will have to answer all this and much more when he meets Mr. Yadav, who has assured the workers that justice will be served.

Prakash sighed and asked Jha, "Who the hell is this Mr. Yadav now?"

"He's the local MLA and also a goon. He has about 10-15 boys who do his dirty work of collecting money for him. We were one of the few companies who paid him nothing. Clearly, he was waiting for us to get in his ambit. Uday and company have given him the perfect opportunity."

"They have even incriminated Joshi. Will he be transferred?"

"That depends on how far the issue goes. If the issue stays within limits and the press stops pursuing it, he will manage it. If they pursue it, he's pretty much had it and we will be in trouble as well."

"What do we do now?"

"We have to go and meet this Yadav."

"This is hell. Let's just pay the money and get rid of these thirteen workers."

"They are not going away that easily, Prakash. This looks like something which might stick with us for a long time."

Prakash and Jha left for Yadav's office. It was a relatively decent building, especially when one compared it to the labour court. There were three floors including the ground floor and apparently, the entire building was the MLA's office.

The ground floor was a gym which looked more like an *akhada* (Indian old-style gymnasium) where ten well-built men were working out. They were Yadav's henchmen and were at his beck and call. The first floor was the administrative department. Rumour had it that though Yadav claimed that it was the admin department, it was the corruption centre of the village. Collections from across all companies were accumulated there. Yadav also had a 'resting' room there where he had his choice of women.

The third floor was where the great politician conducted his affairs. There was a connected office with a door in between. It was quite a modern office for those days. There was a computing machine which had just arrived in India. A man was entering some data into the machine.

Inside was a throne where he would sit and announce his decisions. Yadav believed in having modern day amenities, yet he still believed that he was a king just like in the medieval times. After all, democracy meant the rule of the people's representatives and he was the representative and hence, he was the ruler.

Prakash told Jha, "These computers are not even that common in Bombay. This is the first machine that I have seen in this village. The operator must be really expensive."

Jha gave a sarcastic laugh. "He has money to spend and expenses to show. Where do you think our taxes go? They travel from our pocket to his faster than you can blink your eyes."

Yadav's secretary was a young, good-looking woman who Jha assumed was a regular visitor to Yadav's resting room. She was seated with a notebook taking appointments for Mr. Yadav. Jha told her to inform Yadav that they had come.

She informed Yadav that he had visitors and then told them to wait.

Jha and Prakash waited outside for a full hour. They were finally called in.

Yadav saw them come in and offered them a seat. His office was quite spacious and well maintained. There were expensive paintings on the walls and his desk was made of pure teak wood. There were marble tiles on the floor and there were hardly any cracks noticeable on them. The office was spotless and the chairs were pretty comfortable too.

Jha and Prakash sat down.

Yadav had a demeanour like the Godfather. In a rough tone, he asked, "What do you want?"

Jha replied, "Sir, we want to present our side of the case."

"Do you own the company?"

"No."

"Then I would advise you to shut up."

He then turned to Prakash, "You look like an educated man. Now what do you want?"

"Well, we saw the article about our company. Sir, we would like to give you our side of the story."

"Hmm...I'm not interested in it."

Prakash was silent. He expected that Yadav would at least hear him out. After all, he had consented to meet them. The meeting was not going well and Prakash felt that they had been cornered. He saw that arguing would not serve the purpose and started to get up.

Jha, on the other hand, took matters in his own hands.

He spoke up, "Sir, you have to at least hear us."

Yadav told him calmly, "I request you to go, Mr. Jha."

Jha couldn't digest this and started to speak up again, "Sir, but you have to hear us."

Yadav got up and came towards Jha. Jha stopped talking for a while.

Yadav then slapped him across the face. It was a blatant display of power. There was silence in that room and one could hear the sound of that slap quite clearly. It was an emphatic insult and Jha was rattled.

"You don't know whose office you're in, do you? You are just a measly worker and I run this village. Get out now. This is a slap you will remember all your life. It will teach you to respect people who are more powerful than you."

Jha was stunned. He couldn't fathom what had happened. He walked out with Prakash, dejected. Prakash looked at him. He was embarrassed and had tears in his eye.

They were outside and Prakash stopped Jha. He told him, "I'm happy you showed restraint."

Jha looked at him. "If my mother had been alive, she would have been ashamed of me today. She would rather I killed him and sacrifice myself than be practical and acknowledge his power. Biharis don't look left or right when they act and they definitely don't bother about consequences. They just kill the person who insults them."

Prakash raised his eyebrows and said, "You're hardly a Bihari now. It's been years since you left that place and you hardly go back."

Jha smiled. "It's in my blood."

Joshi was incidentally outside the building. "Did you meet Yadav?"

"Yes, we did."

"That son of a b*** is after my job now. He has called me here. I should have never done a favour for you guys."

Jha stared at him and thought to himself. "What favour is he talking about? He took money for the case."

"Well, my job is gone but your company will not be spared either. You are most probably going to have to pay a huge settlement. He will transfer me but you guys are in big trouble. You think you paid me off. He will take a huge amount for himself and also give out a huge amount to your workers."

When they walked back into the office, Prakash got Jha a glass of water. "You need this. Man, this company is headed to hell and that too just because of thirteen workers."

Sanjay then walked in as well, "Sir, we need some machine oil. We've just run out of it."

He looked at Jha who was quite down and then patted him on the back. "What happened?"

Jha gave him a sad smile. "I just got slapped."

"By whom?"

"Mr. Yadav, the local MLA."

"Why did he slap you?"

"I have no idea. He didn't want me to talk."

"Why did you go to meet him?"

Prakash threw down the newspaper with the article in front of him.

Sanjay took some time to read the entire article. He then turned and looked at Prakash. "Sir, you didn't tell me."

"Well, it didn't concern you. It was about the yarn department. What good would come out of me telling you about this?"

"Well, sir you should have told me about this."

Jha turned to Prakash and said, "You should have told him, let him have gone with you and he would have been the one to get slapped."

Sanjay gave Jha a smug look. "He would never slap me."

"Why? Are you related to him?"

"No."

"Then why would he not slap you? You are obviously more irritating than I am."

"Well..." Sanjay paused a bit to give effect, "He may not be related to me but he knows me. I know how that guy works. He slapped Jha to scare you guys off."

"You think?"

"Yes, he's very theatrical."

"How do you know him?"

"Well, he knows me. Yadav has a textile background. I worked in his company before he got into politics. He shut down the firm because he got a lot of money by selling the land. He then contributed to one of these large political parties to get a seat to contest the assembly elections. He bought votes and became a politician. He would often say politics is the best business. It was his dream to get into politics and become a king."

Prakash's eyes widened, "So, you've worked for Yadav."

"Well, yes. You should take me to talk to him."

Prakash chuckled. "Right. Maybe you should meet him alone. He slapped Jha when the two of us went to meet him. Since he knows you, if we both go, he'll slap me."

"Don't worry. Let's go meet him."

Jha interrupted, "Wait a minute. It might be better to talk to him tomorrow after what happened today."

"Right. Let's meet him tomorrow."

Prakash was slightly pensive when Jha interrupted, "Don't be so worried. We may have finally found a solution because of Sanjay."

"The problem, Jha, is this company is succumbing to politics, union, labour courts and every other thing. We might get out of this problem with Yadav but there will be more politicos, self-proclaimed labour leaders, courts, etc. This location is cursed."

"No location is cursed, Prakash. Companies go through such times and one has to deal with it. You can't just panic at every problem you face. When you are a manufacturing concern, such trade disputes happen and one has to deal with them the best way possible."

Sanjay interrupted, "Sir, this company is the best I have worked for. I will not let this company be ruined because of thirteen people who do not wish to see it grow and flourish. This company is fair to people and that matters a lot to us. We want the firm to survive."

Jha interrupted, "He's right, you know. It's now our *dharma* to work for Dharam."

"You have a way with words, Jha."

"Sometimes, bad things happen to good people."

"Right. Well, let's break it up. We need to work today and get ready for Mr. Yadav tomorrow. Sanjay, I'm going to go meet him wearing a helmet."

"You won't need one, sir. If he hits you, he'll need one."

"Right. Jha, are you still depressed you got slapped?"

Jha stroked his moustache. "Are you joking, sir? In Bihar, we have a saying. Let him do all the injustice he can. The day will come when he will pay. One slap cannot ruffle Mahashankar Jha. I told you right. I'm one of the four most famous things in Bihar."

"Yeah. Crime, politics, Shatrughan Sinha and…"

Jha interrupted him and stroked his moustache. "Jha. Mahashankar Jha."

Prakash smiled back and Jha walked out of his office.

Life Ain't Fair

This was gained by me today, I shall obtain this according to my desires, this wealth is mine and in the future more will also come; the demoniac are deluded by ignorance (16.13).

—Bhagvad Gita

The next day, Prakash and Sanjay left for Yadav's office. They told the secretary that Sanjay wanted to meet him. They knew that he was unlikely to meet Prakash. Yadav kept them waiting for a long time. A lot of other guys walked in and out of the office while Prakash and Sanjay sat outside.

While they waited, Prakash talked to Sanjay about production and other issues in the factory. They finished talking about everything under the sun. After a couple of hours, finally, Yadav called the two of them in.

Yadav was making smoke rings in the air when they walked into his office. He saw Sanjay and immediately asked, "How are you doing, Sanjay?"

Sanjay replied with confidence in his voice, "I am fine, sir. How are you doing?"

"I am doing fine. Ever since I have left that goddamn field of textiles, I have done pretty well for myself."

"Textiles is a difficult job, sir."

"Sanjay, manufacturing has become very difficult to operate now. Information Technology is the next big thing, you mark my words. That is a good field to work in."

"It is certainly a good field to work in, sir."

"Yes. The best business, however, is politics."

"Undoubtedly, sir."

Yadav then turned to Prakash "Instead of bringing that insolent b★★★★, you should have got Sanjay along. We could have sorted out matters then."

"I'm hoping that it's not too late now."

"Right. So tell me your side of the story."

"Well sir, we have almost been held hostage by these thirteen employees. We are now a company of two hundred employees and are growing rapidly. We have always been a fair company. Some vested interests have provoked these thirteen employees and they have gone against the firm. Sir, we have always done what is best for the employees and the firm."

"They are saying that you exceed the stated eight hour shift and are not paying them overtime wages."

"The entire industry works that way. If I don't do that, my cost will spiral and I won't be in a position to compete."

"That doesn't mean you shouldn't do the right thing."

"Sir, you have a textile background. You know it is very difficult to survive if one goes against industry practices."

"They have come to me for help. I can't let them go empty-handed."

"Sir, I don't want them to go empty handed."

"So you're ready to pay them something."

"Sir, we agreed on Rs 65,000 overall to be paid out to these thirteen workers with Mr. Joshi."

"He is a corrupt man. I am going to get him transferred."

"Right, sir. But I request you to look at this situation from our side."

"You know there is nothing in textiles. Why are you in this field?"

"Sir, it is a legacy that I am managing. The firm represents the hopes and dreams of many."

He then chuckled. "You company's name is also Dharam. What a coincidence."

Prakash thought to himself, "You idiot, we named it that way knowing what it stood for. It is not a coincidence."

"Prakash, I understand your situation, but these workers came to me for help and I have to do something for them."

"Right, sir."

"You should pay them two lakhs."

Sanjay then looked at him. "Sir, we can't pay that huge an amount."

"Hmm...Sanjay, for you I will reduce that amount. You should pay them Rs 1.5 lakhs."

"sir…"

"Sanjay, Rs 1.25 lakhs and that is final."

Prakash looked at Sanjay who nodded at him. "Okay, sir. But we would like to take some action against them for inefficiencies after we pay them this amount."

"Don't take any action immediately otherwise they will come back to me looking for justice and then I will be helpless. Give it time and wait for the right moment."

They started to get up when Yadav told Sanjay, "You stay back, Sanjay." He then looked at Prakash. "You may leave."

Prakash left the room immediately and did not question Yadav much lest he got slapped as well. He waited patiently outside for Sanjay for about half an hour.

After half an hour, finally Sanjay came out.

Prakash realized it was not wise to talk about what went on inside the room while they were within the realms of the building. So, he quietly took off with Sanjay.

After they reached a comfortable distance from the building, he turned to Sanjay and asked him, "So, what did he say?"

"What do you think? He asked for money."

Prakash gave a sarcastic smile. "I thought he wasn't corrupt. Joshi was the one who was corrupt."

"I'm sure Joshi tells people Yadav's corrupt and he's the emblem of honesty. Politics is full of chameleons, sir. They change colour and dialogue as they deem fit. For them, anyone they don't know is a danger so they camouflage as much as possible. Why do you think he asked you to leave? I knew him so he bought this issue out only with me in the room."

"If we keep on paying these touts, we will end up paying more than what Uday is asking for."

"Is the question limited to Uday? If you pay them more, all those two hundred employees will stand against you this time with a much larger claim. Once you resolve that, they will find another issue to fight against you. The issue is not even if you're right or wrong. The issue is now about survival. If they find out you're weak, you've had it."

Prakash sighed and asked him, "How much did he ask for?"

"He asked for a lakh and fifty thousand. I got him down to a lakh."

"Okay."

They reached office. Prakash was quite frustrated. Jha walked in.

"Who the hell are these guys fighting? Don't they realize the only beneficiaries in this case are third parties? They are taking us from pillar to pole. Jha, call Uday. Let us try and sort this out with him first."

"Do you think talking to Uday will be of any use? Last time you talked to them, you ended up abusing them. It just made matters worse."

Prakash looked at him and in an irritated tone said, "Just call him."

Jha called Uday down. Sanjay was in the room as well.

Prakash asked Uday, "What do you want?"

"Justice."

"What injustice have we done? Don't you realize that only third parties are benefiting?"

"You are paying for your sins."

"Okay. Even if I've committed sins, you tell me what you want directly now instead of going to someone."

"We deserve sixty thousand each for five years assuming four hours overtime per day for three hundred days for five years and ten rupees an hour. I know my rights. I also want you to pay us proper overtime from now on."

"Uday, you might as well shut down the company."

"Then, let it shut down. I don't care."

Jha moved in front of Uday. "How dare you speak to him like that?"

Uday's eyes were red with anger and so were Jha's. Prakash was in no mood to control them.

Uday shouted loudly, "I will say whatever I want. Your owner is a leech who lives off our blood and you are his pimp."

Jha slapped him hard. Uday recovered and moved to hit Jha. Sanjay intervened and told Uday to go away.

Prakash stared at Uday in disgust. Here was a man who was almost single-handedly holding the entire company to ransom and the worst thing about the situation was that they couldn't do anything about it. The system and laws were like four walls binding them together and any false move would only tighten the screws around them.

Prakash was silent when Sanjay told Jha, "What the hell did you slap him for?"

"How dare he talk to Prakash like that?"

"This situation is only going to get worse with anger, Jha. He is capable of creating a ruckus. We have got Yadav and Joshi on our side. The only thing we need to keep on doing now is to close the doors that he can approach. That is all. Shut down his options and you will shut him out. He is not someone you can dominate."

Prakash turned and told Sanjay and Jha, "I've had enough for the day. I'm going to take off. You guys take care that nothing else happens. If you need me for anything, give me a call."

Both Jha and Sanjay nodded and Prakash walked out of the room.

He went to meet Sushma to change his mood. Their marriage was due in a month. He found solace in the fact that at the end of every difficult day, he would go back home to her daily after a month. God had at least been kind to him by giving him a sensible, loving life partner. Sushma had been a constant source of strength for him through the hell his workplace had become.

They went off for a walk to their usual hangout – the park near Sushma's house. She sensed he was tense so she calmly asked him, "Is everything okay?"

"No, it isn't. I am tired of the constant crap in the company. I don't even know if it's worth it anymore. Maybe, I should go back to my job."

"Why do you feel that way?"

"They will take me back."

"And what happens if something goes wrong there?"

"Sushma, I don't want a lecture of what could and could not go wrong and I'm frustrated with what's going on in this case. They will just not let Dharam run."

"Right."

"He wants the company to be destroyed and he doesn't care. He is a man who cannot be bought and unfortunately he thinks I am the worst possible man on the planet."

"He can't think that about you, Prakash."

"But he does think that way, Sushma. He is impossible to deal with and talk to. He is wrong, but he just doesn't want to admit he's wrong."

"He is an honest person."

"Yeah."

"Have you heard his side?"

"I have. His arguments of us sticking to the book about labour laws are not without basis. But I can't survive if the market does not adopt them. Our costs will go higher than the market and we will be extinct in a year."

"You've not been able to explain that to him?"

"He does not give anyone an opportunity to explain and he just does not trust me. He thinks I am a capitalist who has reached where he has by exploiting people like him. It's like he hates the world and he wants to get back at it. I am the first one he wants to run over. I have half a mind to resign and leave the firm."

Sushma heard him out and spoke after a while, "Prakash, you will not run away from Dharam. Keep on fighting till they kick you out of there. You will not quit. That won't define you as a man. What will define you is staying on and leaving when on a high. You are not leaving Dharam on a dejected note."

Prakash replied in a sad tone, "I am frustrated."

"We all go through that, Prakash. I will be there with you, no matter what. If he wants to take you down, let him. He has to fight you through it and I will back you, no matter what happens. If I have to sacrifice not seeing you for a while, I will do that. I will be by your side. I won't let you give up."

Prakash sighed and said, "I don't see any solution anytime soon. But like you said, it is probably worth fighting to the finish."

"Have you talked to Chand about this?"

"I have. He is at his wits' end. He has never handled production and is completely at a loss."

"We will come out of this. Dharam will come out of this better and stronger."

Prakash looked into her eyes which at that moment showed more conviction in the firm than he had ever seen in anyone's eyes. It was not that she had ever worked in Dharam so she could never really fully grasp the ground reality. Her belief in the company stemmed from her belief in Prakash.

Chand was aging, yet he was very active. He managed most of the sales albeit with the help of an able salesperson whom he gave directions to. The firm would have been fine if not for Uday.

If there was only a way, any way, to sort out the issue with Uday. Prakash so wanted to end the feud. Uday's battle in his head, however, was one of social justice and not one where he would falter, negotiate or surrender easily.

Uday was Dharam's Datta Samant.

A Storm is Coming

The senses, the mind and intelligence are the stronghold of this lust, covering this discrimination this enemy of lust deludes the living entities (3.40).

—Bhagvad Gita

It was the 1990s and India as a country had changed. The prime minister of the time, Narsimha Rao had to contest with extremely low forex reserves and the country was on the verge of bankruptcy. They needed to take tough decisions. At that time, the finance ministry of the country was headed by a Sikh, Mr. Manmohan Singh. He was given a free hand by Narsimha Rao and he moved rapidly towards liberalization.

This was the era that changed the face of India. Foreign brands started to come in. Inflation numbers and income levels shot through the roof. This period would mark the start of a growing middle class. Consumerism started to grow and India moved from being the production back end of the world to a service provider and a viable market for global brands. Satellite television started to make its way into India and one heard that there was something called the internet which would change people's lives forever.

While everything was changing, labour laws were still archaic. There were too many vested interests involved. Multinational companies were starting to make their foray into the country and the hope was that their pressure might force the laws to become more contemporary, equal and practical. That, however, seemed distant.

Dharam had also come a long way into the liberal era. The fabric division was doing really well and so was texturizing. The only department that was bleeding constantly was the twisting department. The workers there hardly worked and on some days left after eight hours claiming that they would work only if they were at par with what the law of the day suggested. They had already disrupted the firm's operations by going to several doors.

While Yadav had been bought out, a new labour officer, Rajendar Kumar came in Joshi's place. Joshi had been found guilty of taking an unfair position in favour of Dharam and had been transferred. The new labour officer was reluctant to show Dharam any favours. Prakash and Jha met him and negotiated the terms of a settlement with Uday but they had to stick to a large number of norms. The shift period had been reduced to eight hours to avoid overtime wages and leaves had to be increased. There were a few areas where Rajendar gave Dharam some leeway but it was in most senses a victory for Uday.

The rebels were not quiet about their achievements. They gloated about it openly to the workers who were involved in weaving and other yarn operations. This was starting to have an impact on the other workers. Sanjay was approached by a few of his weavers who said that the twisting workers seemed to be much better off than them without actually working.

Sanjay went to Prakash's office with a grim look on his face. "I don't know if I'll be able to control them anymore."

"Who are you talking about?"

"The workers are complaining that the twisting guys are getting better working conditions as compared to them. They are also working harder and getting better results yet they are worse off."

"If we change their salaries as well, we might as well close down this firm, Sanjay. We have also changed the work time from twelve to eight hours so they are actually earning lesser than they were earlier.

Rajendar allowed us to shift any worker randomly in any eight hour shift to avoid them working elsewhere on an eight hour shift."

"I know but how does one explain this to them? Uday's group is not silent about what they are getting. They brag about it as if it were their right. You cannot reasonably expect the other workers to ignore this."

Prakash sighed "Sanjay, we have to convince them. We are doing well in the fabric division and they stand to gain if we survive. If they push us to close it down, they will be out of jobs. Everyone stands to lose."

"Sir, they will get influenced. Clearly, the workers in the twisting department have forced their hand and got you to give them what they want. The negotiation has been in their favour. Can't we throw those workers out now?"

"I don't know what to do. We have our backs against the wall. There are so many people involved now who do not want this to die so that these disruptions keep on happening. We can't touch any of these workers as of now."

Jha walked in on the conversation. "What are you guys talking about?"

"Well, the twisting workers have started having an adverse influence on the entire workforce."

Jha said with a noticeable disgust in his voice, "We should throw these people out. They are pure evil."

Prakash sighed. "They are not wrong in asking what the law suggests they ask."

"So you're saying we're wrong?"

"Jha, in a fight it isn't necessary for one side to be wrong and the other to be correct. This is not a *Ramayan* or a *Mahabharat* where you have the devils on one side and the gods on another. We are no gods."

Jha clenched his teeth "We may not be gods but they are definitely devils."

"No. We have failed in getting them to negotiate at an early stage and they have refused to understand our side of the situation."

Sanjay said, "The market is worse. If they go to some other company, they will understand how terrible owners can be."

Prakash smiled. "They're not looking at the market. They're looking at the law."

"The law is different for different people in the market."

"They're being influenced by middle men who pretend they are the guardians of the law when in reality, they are the ones who benefit from such a struggle. They differentiate the law for those who pay for it and those who don't. It's like that story about the monkey and the cats. The cats fight for the cake and the monkey wins."

Jha looked at Sanjay. "Tell them this is a temporary phase. We will over time throw these employees out. Then they will not enjoy anything. These are rebels and we'll draw them out."

"Right now they have got the better of you and if we don't do this quick, I see more joining them. It's clearly more profitable to be on their side than on ours."

Prakash looked at both of them. "Yeah. We have to finish this as quickly as possible."

The only comforting aspect of Prakash's life was his wife Sushma. It was now a year since their wedding. The wedding itself had been quite simple with very few people present.

Whenever Prakash had asked her if she wanted a big wedding, she would say, "I want the marriage to be grand, not the wedding."

The ambience was beautiful even if the wedding was small. It was a serene place overseen by the gods themselves. It was at some distance from the city and secluded from the concrete jungle. There was a small hall nearby which was reserved for the reception.

The temple was decorated with flowers and a sacred fire was lit around which Prakash and Sushma were asked to take seven rounds as was the tradition. The ceremony has been scheduled to take place during late evening when the sun was setting. The fading sunlight fell on the flowers and gave the entire place, a pristine look. There were a few lights to light up the place but Sushma had kept them minimal because the artificial lights would take away from the natural beauty of the surroundings.

She was dressed in a simple red sari without much work on it. She was looking divine and Prakash was dressed in a traditional kurta. He could not take his eyes off his bride. The guests included Prakash's mother and her sister, his brother-in-law, Chand and his daughters with their families, Sanjay and Jha with their wives and a few close relatives.

Each *phera* (round) stood for a commitment that the bride and the groom made to each other. They made a commitment of love, understanding, patience and support to each other that day. The pundit recited the vows in Sanskrit and translated them into Hindi so that both Prakash and Sushma understood what was going on.

The wedding bound two people who were perfect for each other in every way. They hardly fought and in the few instants that they did, the fights never lasted long. It was in all respects a marriage made in heaven.

Sushma would often tease Prakash. "Behind every successful man, there's a woman."

"I am not that successful, sweetheart. You think you're the reason for that too."

Sushma smiled. "You are more successful than you think. Give yourself some credit, Mr. Prakash."

When she smiled, Prakash would feel it was worth it. Every battle has to have an end to make it worth fighting for. This one was probably worth it for ensuring a decent life for Sushma and the workers who were with him.

It was, however, a losing battle. The other workers were starting to feel the bite. It was better at this time to side with Uday than with

Prakash, Jha and Sanjay. If thirteen people could get Prakash to bow down and agree to so many demands, imagine what two hundred people could do.

Dharam was facing the threat of extinction and was headed in the same direction as the mills in Bombay had.

Chand met Prakash one evening at his office in Dharam. "You look worried."

Prakash said, "We won't be able to sustain for long. The workers have started drifting against us. They see what the rebels have got and have realized the benefits in going against us. We may have to consider what happens if we are forced to close shop."

Chand looked at him. "You think we will have to shut down?"

"Yeah."

"The land rates here have increased quite a bit. We won't make a loss even if we shut down."

Prakash stood staring outside at the workers and with a heavy voice replied, "The people working here will lose their jobs. We will lose this firm which was a legacy and a dream. We will not lose money but that's probably the only thing we won't lose."

Chand patted him on the back. "Ironically, the workers will win and yet lose in this process."

Prakash sighed. "Yeah." He stared at the workers outside, knowing there was not much time before the storm created by them engulfed Dharam.

Inferno

Just as fire is covered by smoke, as a mirror by dust and the embryo is covered by the womb; so this knowledge is covered by that lust (3.38).

—*Bhagvad Gita*

The fight with Uday lasted for four years. There were constant tussles, and the number of politicos and union leaders involved were increasing gradually. Every now and then, Uday would find someone who'd help him disrupt the functioning of the firm. He had gone from pillar to post to stop Dharam from functioning normally.

Labour laws in India were developed to avoid exploitation, but hurt hardest in their rigidity. The implementation was done in an adhoc manner. Labour tribunals were akin to the blindfolded image that the Indian legal system portrayed. Every visible wrongdoing was ignored. People who violated the law on a large scale made sure that the right amounts reached the relevant people. As long as someone didn't come and create a ruckus, the company wasn't touched. If a worker complained, he was entertained depending on the underlying company's capacity to pay the tribunal judges and the company was taken to task accordingly.

Dharam continued to function and survive for some time even after the verdict of the battle against Uday went against them. The problem, however, was not that Uday and company got their way. The issue was that they were influencing the other two hundred employees as well. They were being taught the word of the law.

The twisting department was in tatters. Weaving had got competitive but was still profitable. It was getting Dharam by. Prakash was expanding that section of the firm to survive in the market. If twisting had run well, Dharam would have gone big there as well, but it was not meant to be. He had tried to sell off the twisting machinery but was not able to because Uday would go on a strike whenever a buyer came. They forced the company to carry on that operation.

A section of weavers had made their mind up to approach Prakash with a list of their demands. They approached Sanjay who shouted at them. The workers however threatened to agitate if their demands were not met. Sanjay's worst nightmare had started to come true and Dharam was set to go on a downward spiral.

Sanjay went to Prakash. "It's happening. They are threatening to agitate if their demands are not met."

"Well. We expected this, Sanjay. Let them go ahead and approach the politicos. We have decided to shut down the firm here completely if the weaving section goes against us and will submit an application to that effect to the labour office here."

"What? You must be joking!"

"Sanjay, there is no way out now. We are surviving on weaving margins and if they discontinue, this firm is unviable."

"*Sir…*"

Prakash gave Sanjay a defeated look. Sanjay stared at him for a while and knew that nothing was going to come out of convincing Prakash otherwise. There was no other solution but to shut down Dharam if the weaving section went the same way as Uday did. Sanjay went back and somehow convinced the workers to hang on for a while. He also revealed Prakash's plans of shutting shop and was able to push back their demands.

Prakash had found the spirit to somehow carry on even though the problems were steadily increasing. There was an easy way out and Prakash and Chand could have easily resorted to pure play trading again but both wanted to stick it out for some more time, at least until the weavers weren't adamant on them changing their wages.

Sushma was Prakash's biggest strength and was one of the reasons Prakash had been able to stretch the fight as long as he did.

Everything at the personal front was going good for Prakash until Sushma once complained of severe headache. Her listening had also gone down in the past few months and there was a constant pain in her ear.

Prakash took her to the doctor who recommended she be admitted immediately for some tests. He got her admitted to one of the best hospitals in Bombay. It was a huge hospital with about fifty beds which were quite large for that day and age. Sushma was admitted to a single bed room.

After many tests, it was diagnosed that Sushma had a brain tumour. Prakash was devastated when he heard of the results. It was as if his life had been taken away from him. There were some further tests to be done to check if it was benign or malignant. Prakash entered Sushma's room that day looking quite disappointed.

Sushma realized something was up. "What happened, Prakash? What did you find out?"

Prakash said with a pensive voice, "Nothing, everything's fine. Everything is going to be okay."

She smiled and took him close. "Even though I know it is not, Prakash, you have to believe it will be. You are going to be okay even if I am not there with you."

"You are always going to be there with me. There is nothing for me beyond you. I have no one."

"Prakash, you have a huge family. Your mother, sister and the entire work force of Dharam."

"You are all I have and all that matters for me."

"Hey, I am always going to be there for you."

"Everything is fine. It has to be. You and I are meant to be together. Behind every successful person, there is a woman. You have to be behind me for me to survive."

Sushma looked at Prakash. "I thought you were not successful."

"I am not without you backing me up. With you, everything is fine."

She smiled and then looked at Prakash. "We don't know if it is benign or malignant yet. You never know. I may still have time."

The doctor took the relevant samples and sent both of them home.

Chand was waiting at home. He was in a state of panic. Prakash wondered whether he had found out about Sushma.

As soon as they reached, Chand held Prakash's hand and said, "We need to leave immediately."

Prakash looked at him and said, "Why? What happened?"

Chand was in tears. "Dharam has caught fire, Prakash. Everything is finished."

Prakash was stunned. Sushma was too shocked to react. They stared at Chand for a while. Prakash helped Sushma to the bed so that she could relax. He then immediately took the car and left for the factory.

Prakash was silent the entire way. He was blank. This chapter of his life had taken a cruel turn. He had received two rude shocks in a day. It seemed as if everything was slipping away from him. He had hit rock bottom.

They reached Dharam after a long drive. Sanjay and Jha were standing in front of the burning unit. The entire unit was in flames. The fire had engulfed almost all of the stock and was so huge that the structure had collapsed on the machines. The firemen had taken time to come to the site and the fire had spread by then to such an extent that the damage was already done. One could see the flames engulfing all the sections.

Hoses of water were being aimed at the fire. The workers had got buckets of water and were throwing them on the burning structure. Sanjay and Jha could not believe what they were seeing. They were trying to salvage the stock. The fire was so big that the flames stretched almost twenty feet high. Firemen were on ladders with their hoses pointed towards the fire.

Meanwhile, the workers were trying to salvage some of the stock. Most were in tears and trying hard to save as much as they could. There was a truck which was called for to take any stock that was salvaged to a nearby godown which belonged to Prakash's friend.

People from other factories in Vasantgam also came to the site as soon as they heard the news. There were loud voices in the background,

"Save that carton from burning."

"God, this is a large fire."

"May God have mercy on the man who owns this factory."

"The owners of the factory are ruined."

"Throw some water in that area."

"Lucky that no one was inside the factory when the fire happened."

These voices were firmly embedded in Prakash, Sanjay and Jha's unconscious minds. It was horrifying to see Dharam burn down like this.

Meanwhile, Uday also arrived at the site. He was off duty that day. He came as soon as he heard Dharam was on fire. Uday saw the sight and assumed that the owner deserved it. This was his punishment. God had showed him who was right. Dharam deserved to be engulfed in those flames.

He was smiling and Jha saw that. Jha left everything and moved towards him. He slapped him hard on his face. Uday's eyes grew red and he started to hit Jha back. The other workers saw this and they moved to separate the two of them.

Sanjay also moved towards Jha and told him, "What the hell are you doing? Don't you realize Dharam is burning? Why are you focusing on this idiot? Let us salvage whatever we can."

Jha sighed and started crying, "From the day I started twisting, I have been only a bad omen for Prakash. I wish I had burned in this fire."

Sanjay patted him on the back to calm him down. They then got up again and started helping with the stock.

Meanwhile, a few workers got buckets full of water and were using them to douse the fire. There was commotion all around with water being thrown from various places to douse the fire. The fire brigade was able to bring it under control after many hours.

Both Prakash and Chand stood there in shock. Everything around them seemed ruined. The structure at places had collapsed on the machines and they were damaged. The stock was almost all gone. The fire had engulfed everything.

Chand started to cry and shouted loudly, "Everything is finished. We are finished." The workers watched their owner who had always maintained his composure in front of them break down. Prakash's eyes were full as well.

Prakash managed to maintain his composure and moved towards the trucks. He started to shiver as he moved towards the fire. He pushed the workers to collect stock from wherever it was feasible.

As time passed, the intensity of the fire started to subside. There was smoke all around and the fire brigades ran out of water.

One of the fire brigade members came towards Prakash and commented, "We have not seen a large one like this from a pretty long time. The damage has been severe. We're very sorry for your loss."

It was the scariest day in the life of Prakash and Chand. Their life's work was in ruins and there was nothing they could do about it. Dharam was no more. It seemed like their worst nightmare had come true.

After the last few flames were brought under control and the last truck had moved away, Prakash leaned against the wall to grasp his breath. Sanjay and Jha came towards him.

He looked at them with tears in his eyes. "I guess this was the end of this company. Maybe this was meant to be. This is how the story is supposed to end."

Sanjay hugged his owner and couldn't stop himself from crying, "I'm sorry, sir."

Jha stared at him blankly and asked, "Is this the end?"

Prakash sighed and looked towards him. "Looks like it. I guess this is God's will."

"This can't be the end. Don't we have insurance? We will rebuild it."

He sighed and looked at Jha. "Claims take time. We will file a claim to recover the loss but I don't know if I have it in me to rebuild this. Chand is becoming old, Uday has become a recurrent problem and Sushma has been diagnosed with a tumour. I don't see any reason to work anymore."

Chand was nearby and overheard him. "Sushma has a tumour?"

"Yes. I guess God wanted us to experience all the crap he could throw at us at the same time. Anyway, if something happens to her, I really don't care what I do. There is nothing left."

Chand immediately replied, "Don't say that, Prakash. Ancient Indians worshipped fire because it cleanses as well as destroys. This can't be it for Dharam. I will not die knowing my legacy is no more."

"Every sign says not to build this firm again. Uday, the fire and the tumour are all indications by God that we are done. Maybe, this is his way of telling us to move on and do something else."

"No. Prakash, we cannot let this be the end of this institution."

Prakash looked at him and said, "Chand, I am done with this. I don't care what happens from here on. I will get the insurance guy here and get a survey done so we can get the claim which we can use for ourselves. After that, I want nothing to do with this firm. Why should I work hard for employees who don't care? Who am I building a legacy for? I don't have a child and the woman who I love the most is about to die. The way I see it, I am going to be left all alone working for a firm who no one gives a rat's ass for."

Chand was about to reply when Sanjay said, "Sir, let us at least inform the insurance company and get that process started immediately."

Chand then turned and asked Prakash, "Are the machines damaged?"

"Seems so."

He looked at Sanjay and said, "Can you check the extent of damage?"

Sanjay moved in the building. He had to mind his step because the shed was falling down at places. He took a close look at all the machines.

Meanwhile, Prakash went to a neighbouring office and informed the insurance company about the debacle. The estimated loss was about one and a half crores including the loss to the building, machinery and stock. He gave them a rough estimate. The survey was to happen the next day early morning so Prakash decided to stay back. He was worried about who would take care of Sushma while he was there but he had no choice. It was already very late and there was no way he would make it back in time for the insurance survey.

He went back to the site and Sanjay and Jha were right there. He reached up to them and told them to go home.

Sanjay replied with moist eyes, "No, sir. I will not leave. I won't get any sleep. I will have nightmares. Even while I am awake, I can hear those voices shouting around me. My mind is in chaos."

Jha looked at him and said, "Sir, please decide to rebuild this institution. Dharam needs to carry on."

Sanjay added, "The machines are fine and can be restarted with minimal investment. We just need your support and guidance and we will get them up and running."

Prakash ignored their requests and said, "You guys need to go home. You need to be back here early tomorrow because the surveyors are going to be here. You need to be present as witnesses. Also, you are going to have to keep Uday and the other rebels away from here."

"Okay."

Prakash left for a hotel room. He had sent Chand back home with a driver.

When he reached the hotel, he immediately called Sushma.

"Are you okay?"

"Yes, I am fine but I have been worried all this while. What happened to Dharam?"

"It has burnt down completely. I don't know if I want to run it anymore. I'm done. I will however fight for the claim. There's a survey tomorrow and I have stayed back for it."

"Don't say that. Dharam is an outcome of your and Chand's dreams. Don't give up on them now."

"They don't matter anymore, Sushma. Did the doctor call back with the test results?"

"No, he didn't. Don't worry about me. You stay there and get Dharam up and running."

"I don't care about the firm. I care about you."

"I am there for you. Don't worry, Prakash. You take care and make sure you have something to eat there, okay?"

"Yeah, I will. I love you."

"I love you too."

Prakash kept the phone down. He stopped his mind from thinking. The last two days had brought an end to almost all the aspects of his life that he cared about.

Life was about to take a starker turn for Prakash. Back home in Bombay before the conversation with Prakash, Sushma was informed about the test results. The tumor was malignant and its growth was extremely rapid. Sushma had very little time left.

A Lifeless Carcass

Death is certain of that which is born. Birth is certain of that which is dead. Therefore, you should not lament over the inevitable (2.27).

—Bhagvad Gita

He was completely lost that day. She was sick, very sick. Her tumour had grown rapidly. Prakash was hardly able to focus on Dharam. Sushma was his primary and only concern and he was losing her and could do nothing about it. He had cried every day of his ill-fated life since he found out about Sushma's tumour being malignant.

The soulless politicos, corrupt bureaucrats and the dirty system had not bothered Prakash that much. These things had not broken him as much as Sushma's tumour had.

Sushma was sleeping peacefully with Prakash by her side. Prakash sat there for hours just looking at her. Sushma had taken priority over everyone else. She got up from her sleep and Prakash told her, "You're fine."

She looked at him smiling with tears in his eye, "I know I am dying, sweetheart."

"No, you are not."

"Prakash, you need to accept it, keep me happy in my last days and let me go in peace."

"If you leave me, I will kill myself."

"No, you will not. You will rebuild that what you have lost.'

Prakash's eyes were in tears. "For whom? I don't care about it anymore. It's cleaned out by God's will. The company's burnt. He's taking you from me. Why should I work?"

Sushma smiled. "You will fight to give your life meaning. Dharam is your life. You will not quit this way. You will see me in the new structure that you rebuild. Promise me that you will give me a rebirth. The new Dharam will have a new soul. I will be in it."

He gave her a hug and said, "You will not leave me. I won't let you go."

He hardly went to the site those days. He had submitted an insurance claim and there was a deadline of two months to submit the relevant documents. For a month, he did nothing. He just sat by Sushma's bed crying. Chand tried to get him to come to the firm and complete the claim documents but Prakash did not care. He just didn't. Chand tried to complete filing the documents himself with the help of Sanjay but he realized it was impossible without Prakash. Prakash was the only one who had the right amount of technical and financial input needed to complete the claim documents and unfortunately, he just didn't care. His life, according to him, was to be over with Sushma.

Jha and Sanjay, meanwhile, kept the team together. Chand had started trading and he kept paying the team wages at home. More than two hundred employees got money sitting at home because Chand did not want anyone to go without money.

The key to Dharam, however, lay in Prakash coming back. Prakash had given up on everything and he was watching Sushma die. Dharam was dying a slow death on the other side.

Sushma was fast losing her faculties. The tumour damaged her ability to hear first because the ear apparently is the first organ it affects. It then destroyed her capability to see and then move.

When Sushma was almost on the verge of her death, Prakash got her admitted to the hospital. She was on life support and Prakash was in the room alone at night. He had not gone home at all. Chand was busy with his work and there was no one to tell Prakash to go home.

"You know, we shouldn't spend so much now. We will need the money when we build a family."
"I don't care, Sushma. You should buy whatever you want. We have enough money to take care of four or five children."
"Prakash, we are not having four or five children."
"How many should we have then?"
"I don't know, but we are definitely not having so many children."
He lifted her up and said, "I don't care if we have one, two, three, four or even none as long as I am with you. I love you."
"Let me down. I will fall."
"I won't let you."
"Promise me you won't let me fall and not physically. I don't want to fall from your eyes, your hopes and your dreams. If I leave before you, you will remember me by keeping a symbol that stands for all that I had."

Prakash got up from a daze. Sushma was on life support in front of him. The life was slowly being sucked out of her and the death was slow. It was as if the spirit was locked inside her body begging for release and the only force holding her back was Prakash's will. The tussle was destroying all and everything around it.

The night Sushma passed away, Prakash was by her side holding her hand. He held her fist and almost felt her leaving the body.

The next day, more than three hundred people showed up to bid farewell to Sushma out of which two hundred were employees of the firm which was dying as slow a death as Sushma had. They were soon going to be out of jobs and a means of livelihood and they had come to the funeral to check if there was any life left in the soldier who had manned the forts of the institution that had fed them for long.

When Prakash took her body to the funeral home, every step killed him. While people around him were chanting, he was staring at the empty space in front of him. He was all alone from here on and devoid of any purpose in his life.

Prakash was in tatters. His hands were shaking as he followed the instructions of the pundit. Chand was standing right behind him as were Prakash's sister, his sister's husband and Chand's daughters. They were trying hard to hide their sorrow and to console Prakash but he was beyond any consolation.

He lit the fire to her pyre and shouted and cried inconsolably. She was no more. The body also was no more. There was nothing left of her. He watched the fire till it died out. He wanted to remember this sight. It was the maximum pain he had experienced in his life.

The third day, he went to collect her ashes. Chand went along with him.

They collected the ashes and put it in a bowl. He then told Prakash, "I want you to join office after tomorrow."

Prakash was stunned. "I am not going to work."

"So, what are you going to do then?"

"I am going to spend my remaining days doing arbitrary things. I am not going to work again in that godforsaken company. Tell that b★★★★★ Uday he has won. I have nothing to lose anymore. There is no reason for Dharam to exist anymore. Who am I working for? I have no wife or child. I am done."

"I don't care, Prakash. Dharam is not a dead institution. It is what we both have worked for."

Prakash shouted loudly, "I don't care. I am not going to work in that firm anymore. I am done. You take the share."

"I don't want your goddamn share. I want you."

Chand grabbed Prakash's hand angrily. He took the bowl in his hands and took Prakash in a car to the station. They waited there for a train.

Prakash stared blankly, not caring about where he was being taken.

What followed was a three hour journey to Vasantgam. They reached the village and Chand called Sanjay and Jha to the burnt down site.

They immediately came to the site. Prakash stood at the site and stared at the rubble around him.

He turned to Sanjay and Jha who looked at him both with pity and expectation.

He then looked at Chand and said, "They will all find other jobs. I am done with Dharam."

Chand had also called a few of the workers to the site. He pointed at one of them and said, "You want purpose? This is your goddamn purpose. You have to fight to carry this firm through for them. You have to take it through this rough time and bring it out of this mess so that they can feed their wives and children. They depend on this land and on you."

Prakash broke down and started crying like a child. He kept on weeping till he was completely out of energy.

Chand let him cry. "She's not gone yet. She believed in you and this firm. She is with you and is your source of strength."

"She was the thing that mattered the most to me."

Chand took some ash out from the bowl and sprinkled it on the land. "Now this is what will matter most to you because her ash is now part of this land. This is your religion now. *This institution is your Dharam.*"

The ash settled down on the debris. Chand had made Sushma the foundation of Dharam.

Agneepath

He whose mind is unaffected by misery or pleasure and is free from all bonds and attachments, fear and anger, is man, of steady wisdom and decisive intellect (2.56).

—Bhagvad Gita

"Good morning, Sushma." Prakash kissed her slightly on her forehead.

"You know my favourite time is when you get up in the morning and wake me up like that. It makes me feel alive. The moment where I know that your love is the most important for me."

"God has blessed me. I must be his favourite child. He gave me the best partner possible. I love you so much."

"Now go get me my cup of tea."

Prakash started to get up to go to the kitchen. Sushma smiled and held his hand, "I was joking. I'm going to make both of us some tea. You relax."

"Why? I can make tea as well. It doesn't affect my position in this household. I like to cook for you."

Sushma smiled and looked at him lovingly. She then gently kissed him on his forehead. "I get scared that all of this will go away one day. I just love you so much I can't live without you."

"You'll never have to. We will have a long and happy life together."

Prakash suddenly woke up. This was among the many memories that Sushma had left him with. They had haunted him every moment from her death.

In fairy tales, one often reads about a resurrection stone that can be used to revive a dead person. If there was one loss Prakash wanted to reverse, it was that of Sushma. With Sushma's death, he had lost purpose.

It was the heaviest loss to bear. You wake up next to your partner, plan your life with her, work hard to make those plans work and all of a sudden, she just leaves you alone.

A few days after Sushma's death, Jha decided to take the day off and visit his boss in Bombay. His boss was at home that day. All the relatives and other associated people had moved on. He was all alone on a sofa with the television set in front of him.

He had tears in his eyes and a blank expression staring into space. The voice coming out from the television was a good distraction, otherwise there was only silence around him.

Jha knocked on his door. "Sir, can I come in?"

"Yeah, please do."

"How are you doing?"

"How do you think? I just feel hollow inside."

Jha sighed and then opened a bag that he had got, "I've got alcohol."

"Are you joking? I haven't drunk a drop in my life."

"Sir, you just said you are dead. Technically, you are still not having it in this life."

"You know what, pour me a drink. Maybe, I can drink till I'm dead."

"Well, that was not the purpose of getting this drink but whatever works for you."

Jha opened the bottle of whisky and poured both of them a glass each. He poured some soda in both and said, "I never thought I will drink with my boss, you know."

Prakash gulped his drink down, coughed for a while because it tasted sour, "God, what the hell is this?"

Jha said, "Give it a while. It takes time to settle in."

"Right. I am feeling a bit dizzy."

"Here, have one more, sir. My boss is finally drinking." Jha poured his boss one more drink.

"I ain't your boss now, you know. I am not working in that goddamn company anymore."

"Chand is paying us all sitting at home with the trading profits that he is generating. He wants us to continue working. He believes you will come around. You will still be my boss."

"No. Old men are generally insane."

"You are calling the man who got you here insane?"

"I am a couple of drinks down. Why are we talking about him anyway?"

"Right. Let's talk about her then."

"We wanted to have two children. We had picked out names – Divya and Vivek. We wanted a boy and a girl."

"Right."

"I wanted to build Dharam so that my boy would carry forward my legacy and Sushma and I would have a child whose future was taken care of. We wanted to raise him with all the security in the world."

"Right."

"But she died. She left me."

He then broke down. Jha hugged him and let him cry for a while.

"Did she love you?"

"A lot."

"Did she know she was going to die?"

"Yes."

"Did you ever talk about what she wanted you to do once she was gone?"

He looked at Jha and said, "Yeah."

"What?"

"She wanted me to rebuild Dharam."

"Did you tell Chand sir this?"

"No."

"So, he threw the ashes on Dharam himself?"

"What are you trying to get at, Jha?"

"Sir, alcohol gives clarity. I know memories are clogging your head right now. I think that if she had her way, you would be doing something else. Chand sir inadvertently did the same thing,"

"I don't care."

"Right. I think if there is anything material that will keep her alive now, it is Dharam. All the signs are pointing towards that, sir."

Prakash looked at him.

"Sir, have another drink. You should drink till you're dead today."

He made Prakash another drink.

Prakash gulped it down, "Why are you trying to kill me?"

"The old Prakash is dead, sir. He had two things in his life and they have both been taken from him. I want to see if I can bring out a new man here. So, I am trying to kill the old one."

Prakash got up and started to walk around the house. He started touching his head which was spinning round and round. Jha had given him three strong drinks. That was quite a bit to handle for a man who did not drink at all.

He then turned to Jha, "I want her back."

"That is not going to happen, sir. You need to build Dharam now to immortalize her."

Prakash paused and then said, "What about Uday? I am done with all of that crap. Those dirty politicians, labour court judges and bureaucrats. I don't want to fight that battle."

Jha had a few tears in his eyes, "Sir, you were fighting for Dharam. That was a battle to save an institution that you cared about. When you see Sushma in that institution, you substitute care for passion. They could have won earlier. They will not win now. You are not fighting to save Dharam. You are now fighting to save what Dharam stands for and that is Sushma, your wife. As far as I am concerned, that battle will be over before it starts."

Prakash was silent. He did not respond.

Jha continued, "You know I have studied only till the eighth standard. We were taught this poem by the great Harivanshray Bachchan – *Agneepath*."

Prakash turned. "Yeah. I've heard that one. It talks about struggle in life, right?

Jha responded, "Yeah. It is about struggle."

Tu naa thakega kabhi, tu naa thamega kabhi, kar shapath, kar shapath, kar shapath...Agneepath, Agneepath, Agneepath (You will never stop, You will never halt, You will never turn, Take this oath, take this oath, take this oath (Walk on the) Path of Fire, (Walk on the) Path of Fire, (Walk on the) Path of Fire).

Death is Only the Beginning

Just as a person casts off worn out garments and puts on others that are new, even so, the embodied soul casts off worn out bodies and takes on others that are new (2.22).

—Bhagvad Gita

When you are down in the dumps, there are two possible conclusions. The hit may be deep enough to finish off any chance of revival. The other is you try to come back. If you make it out of a pit, you generally come back stronger and better than before.

Prakash mustered the strength to go back to Dharam the next day. Chand had started the debris clearance after receiving the go-ahead from the insurance team. He was losing steam. He was old and had never looked at any aspect of manufacturing. Sales were less tedious than manufacturing and he had become used to sales.

When Prakash was staring at the machines clearing out the debris, a hand tapped him from behind.

"Sir, you're back."

Sanjay and Jha were standing behind him.

"Sanjay, how are we doing?"

"Well, Chand said the insurance will take time. We haven't fired anyone but have lost about 20-30 percent of the workforce."

Prakash looked at him and gave a sarcastic laugh. "I guess even paying them while they're not working doesn't ensure loyalty."

Jha said, "No, sir. The people who have left could have stayed on but few refused to stay on and become a burden on the firm."

"Right. Has Uday and company left?"

"No, sir. Not one of them has left. They feel the company still owes them so if it revives, they will get their jobs."

"Great. So even if we struggle to get Dharam back somehow, there will always be an Uday to deal with."

"Right. There is one change though."

"What?"

"The sympathy wave among the other workers apart from those thirteen spoilt ones is now completely with you and the politicos, it seems, have backed off."

"How do you know the politicos and union guys are no longer involved?"

"Well, they are no longer interested. They figured that the company is ruined for good so there's nothing much to be gained."

"Right."

"So we first build Dharam and then negate these thirteen one by one. This time, we do it in a razor-sharp manner so that none of them have any door to knock on."

Prakash looked at them and said, "Yeah."

Jha kept on staring at him and couldn't stop a few tears. He then gulped and said, "Sir, are you back for good?"

Prakash paused for a moment and then looked at the debris. He stared at it for a while and then said, "Let's bring her back from the dead."

Sanjay interrupted, "Sir, this is Dharam, not Sushma."

Jha said almost immediately looking at Sanjay in anger, "They are now one and the same."

Prakash called Chand, "Chand, have you got any update from the insurance authorities."

Chand realized what was going on and immediately said, "They will give us an on-account payment. But the full and final realization might take some months."

"Right. Are the documents complete?"

"Well, they have some queries before they prepare the final statement. I think the surveyors might also be expecting something. You should go visit them."

"Okay."

He then turned to Sanjay, "Have you taken a look at the machines?"

"I have. We can get them started one by one. But where do we start them?"

"We take a place on rent and rebuild this in the meantime. We have orders in hand and have to complete them."

Jha then said, "There is a place we can get on rent."

"How quickly can you get the machines running?"

"The damage varies from machine to machine. My judgement is that at least 20 of the 50 machines can be started immediately. 20 might start in a month and the remaining 10 might take a full month more."

"Great. Let's take a place on rent and get started."

Jha said, "Let's go visit that guy. Dharam, after all, needs to come back."

"Let's also call the architect. The debris should be fully out in a week's time. Let's start the construction as soon as we can."

Jha smiled. "Back with a bang."

"Let's just say back with a mission. I have to revive this firm and get it running. Like you said, there's more to Dharam now for me that there was ever before."

Jha and Prakash took off to meet the owner of the rental place. The owner was a Muslim man named Insaaf Ali Khan. His office was in a godown cum shop in the industrial centre. There was waste yarn outside his godown in gunny bags. The office was just a room with a table, a chair and an almirah on the side.

Insaaf Ali Khan was a well-built man with a moustache longer than Jha's. He saw them coming and stood up immediately.

Jha started to introduce him. "This is Prakash, the owner of Dharam. Our company recently…"

Insaaf interrupted him, "I know who he is. I have dealt with him before."

"You have."

"Yes. I bought waste yarn from you. Your team was the cleanest even in dealing with waste yarn purchasers such as me. The other companies always try to cheat me."

Prakash then started to say, "Dharam, my firm, was burnt down in a fire."

"I know. Don't worry. Allah is with you. He is with everyone who is just and fair. This is but a temporary setback." He then pointed at Jha and said, "You also have cartoons like him on your side."

Jha looked at him and said, "What Mr. Insaaf? I am not a cartoon character."

Insaaf then patted Jha on his back. He was so strong that Jha almost bent down with the impact.

Insaaf then looked at him and said, "Only the moustache is big. No real strength in you."

Jha said, "Mr. Insaaf, my strength lies in my heart."

"But that heart also looks very small."

Jha and Prakash smiled. "We wanted to take your place on rent."

"Okay. No problem."

"What will be the rent?"

"Two rupees per square feet."

Jha immediately said, "Sir, reduce it by a little bit at least."

Prakash interrupted him "No, no. We will pay two rupees per square feet."

Jha stared at him. Prakash had not negotiated at all. He could have easily got Insaaf down to one-and-a-half rupee per square feet."

Insaaf then looked at Prakash and smiled. "I liked that about you then as well. You are smarter than the others who negotiate for petty things. You want something else."

"Yes."

"What?"

"You have to give us the first floor for free so that I can start my yarn twisting machines there."

Insaaf narrowed his eyes and looked at him, "You know that area would go at 1.5 rupees per square feet at a minimum."

"I am paying you two rupees for the bottom."

"But, you still stand to gain. Smart man." He then hit Jha on his back again. This time Jha fell down. "Learn something from your owner."

Jha looked at him and said, "If I get out of your office alive and healthy, I will try to learn."

"Done. Also, there is no need for you to give me a deposit. I trust you completely. You have to give me one month's notice."

"I will give you the notice. Thank you, Mr. Insaaf."

He then tried to shake hands. Insaaf pulled him close and hugged him. "You will see that there will be a bigger company in the place of the one burnt down. This is just a temporary thing."

"Yes."

He then turned to hug Jha who moved away, "You are too strong for me."

Insaaf smiled and moved towards Jha and hit him again. "Haha... You are very funny. I like a funny man."

"If you like me, why are you hell bent on killing me?"

"Oh, don't worry. I won't kill you."

"Okay."

"Do you want to put a board outside the company?"

"No," Prakash replied.

"You don't want to do that. The current board outside says RR Industries. Are you sure you don't want to replace it?"

"Yes. I'm sure. Dharam is a name given to that site which burnt down. It had an aura. I believe only that place can be Dharam again. The place you own will always be RR."

"I respect that, Prakash."

"Thank you."

Jha and Prakash walked out of the place and went back to Dharam. Jha then turned to Prakash. "We haven't seen the building yet. How do you even know it had an additional floor?"

"When he had purchased yarn from me, he had talked about his building and how big it was. He talked about it being the same size as Dharam except the additional twisting section area."

"You are an amazing man, sir."

"I know that. He told you to learn from me, remember, while he was in the process of maiming you."

"My back hurts from his blows, but they were for you, so no harm done."

"No, they were not. They were an expression of his love towards you."

"Sir, I am married with two kids who you have put through school."

"The way he treated you, I don't think that would be an obstacle."

Jha teasingly said, "What, sir? You will say anything you want!"

Prakash then responded, "What, Jha? You will do anything you want!"

"Let's get a lifting machine and get things moving then. We have to move the machines out."

"Yes. Let's do that immediately and get things in operation."

There was a moment of silence. Prakash then spoke, "You know things have been happening so fast today that I haven't even got time to think. This has been the first day since her death that I haven't reflected on it."

Jha stood silent and saw a tear coming from Prakash's eyes.

He then said, "You can't bring her back but a wise old man once told me death is only the beginning. Dharam's destruction and Sushma madam's death is the beginning for this firm. It deserves to be revived."

Prakash looked at him and sighed, "Death is only the beginning."

Resurrection

Never was there a time when I did not exist, nor you, nor all these kings; nor in the future shall any of us cease to be (2.17).

—*Bhagvad Gita*

Uday's wife had seen him lazing around from a long time. "You haven't been going to work, have you?"

Uday replied, "Are you concerned I spend too much time at home?"

"No, but earlier you used to work and earn. Now you sit and earn."

"That b*****'s factory got burnt down. He finally got what he deserved."

"You hate him so much yet he's giving you your salary even when you're doing nothing. Isn't that a good gesture?"

"No. He will lose all of us if he doesn't and he doesn't want that to happen. Who will restart his bloody company then?"

"Okay."

Uday then sobered down a bit, "He also lost his wife."

His wife looked at him with a sad face. "I pity him. He's lost everything at once."

Uday did not respond to that. He was also in two minds whether Prakash really deserved all that he got. He was, however, committed to his hatred and his mission of getting just and fair returns for the employees as per the written rule. After all, labour laws were meant to be implemented and Prakash had not done that.

He had also gotten used to the free money. Sloth was a luxury he had never had in his life. He had to hold on to his hatred against Prakash to justify the slothfulness. He was getting enough money to run the house, there was no work to do and he spent his time lazing around the house.

Meanwhile, Prakash had gradually shifted the machines to RR. He had also started the clean-up of the premises so that they could start the construction.

Sanjay and Jha got most of the machines started in no time. Chand already had orders pending which he was handling via job work. It was a tough task since there was limited control over the manufacturing process. They had no choice because they had to keep the revenue ticking and meet their obligations.

Once the machines were working, the workers started coming back. Jha called back his employees including Uday and company. While most of the workers were happy to be back since they had been insecure about their jobs, some of them had become used to being paid without work. It was as if they were in some social security scheme.

Prakash had instructed Jha earlier not to start the twisting machines. When Uday and company came back, they saw that the twisting machines were damaged and they had not been repaired. Uday walked up to Jha, "The machines are not working. What work do you expect us to do?"

Jha immediately shot back, "You will have to work as helpers."

Uday's eyes lit up, "What? We will never work as helpers."

Helpers were unskilled workers and the mandatory minimum wages for them were lesser than skilled workers as defined in the Indian labour laws.

Jha sighed, "So the thing is that there is no work here. If you've got a few lakhs, hand it over to us so we can buy new ones. We will not, however, pay your salary for the days you don't work."

Uday was livid. He realized he had been played. He moved forward to hit Jha but Jha slapped him hard. He took Uday by surprise. Uday wanted to get up to hit him but a few of Jha's men immediately stood behind him.

Jha shouted loudly, "You stay within your limits. We have tolerated your drama enough. Uday, there is still time. Take stock of your life before you ruin it. If you won't, I'll ruin your life myself."

Prakash and Sanjay were watching the drama from a distance.

Sanjay smiled. "Looks like Jha finally got his revenge."

Prakash looked at him. "You've got to admit that the man has a lot of strength."

"Ha. What strength? His antics can only work against Uday. He would not dare and try such stunts on me."

"He's your wife, Sanjay. He can torture you any way he wants."

Jha meanwhile stepped away leaving Uday on the ground.

Sanjay turned and saw the machines running and commented to Prakash, "Now it feels like Dharam is back."

Prakash stared back at him and said, "No it is not back yet."

Jha smiled and said, "Let's visit the site and see how work is going on there."

They took off to see how the construction work was progressing at the site. The debris had been cleaned and the place was razed to the ground looking like a barren field.

Prakash looked at the place and said, "I never realized that there was so much land."

"Yeah, the place seems so barren. It's hard to believe we worked here."

Jha looked at Sanjay. "Right. It just seems like yesterday that I kicked your ass in the company."

"Jha, you are half my size. The only thing that you have that is bigger than mine is your moustache."

Jha stroked his moustache, "And my heart."

Prakash looked at them and smiled. He had actually missed this bickering.

Jha saw him smiling and pointed at Sanjay, "I knew this cartoon character would make you smile."

"What did you say, Veerappan?"

"Did you just call me Veerappan?"

"Yes."

Jha stroked his moustache and raised his voice slightly, "The name is not Veerappan. It is Jha....Mahashankar Jha."

Prakash stared at the land in front of him. His memories of the factory when it was running also related to a time where he was happy with Sushma. Her death had been so sudden. How could someone so full of life leave so soon?

Uday and team were sluggish at work as usual. Uday had got back to his job of discussing the injustices meted out on the Dharam team in the past. There was one change though. Just before the fire, a lot of the weaving personnel had started to drift towards his thought process. Now, they were totally against it. They were glad that Prakash was back.

Prakash and Chand had ensured they were fed at home. They had done all in their power to keep the firm going. A unit nearby had shut down with all the workers jobless. Looking at that, workers feared for their jobs and further turned against Uday's thought process. They started threatening him to stop plotting against Dharam because they believed his actions might shut the firm down.

Meanwhile, the insurance process was taking its own time. Prakash had taken over the follow-up job from Chand and ensured there was no gap in the data submitted to the insurance firms.

He made it a habit to visit the surveyor frequently. The surveyor was a Gujarati, Mr. Ratanlal Shah.

Mr. Shah was very concerned with some of the figures that

Prakash had presented. He called him to his office one day. Prakash went over in what was to be one of many visits. Shah was stationed in a posh building in Mumbai and was apparently the common surveyor of many insurance companies.

His office was quite small, around 400 square feet and had very few people – Mr. Shah and a couple more. There were a couple of computer terminals and a lot of files in a rack. As soon as Prakash came, Shah called him in.

"Mr. Prakash, how are you doing?"

"Not very well, sir. We are trying hard to reconstruct the building and we need the insurance funds urgently."

"Right. The total loss shown is Rs 80 lakhs. I don't think it was that huge."

"Sir, we have been over this many times now. I have shown you all the documents pertaining to this. Our documents are transparent."

"But I still don't think you are on the mark."

So, what do you want me to do, sir?"

"Hmm…"

Prakash understood what the silence meant. He immediately said, "Sir, we would be glad to avail of your help and if there is anything we could do for you, let us know."

"Are you offering me a bribe?"

"No, sir. We just want to thank you for all the hard work that you are doing."

"Hmm…"

There was silence for a while before Shah spoke up. "Listen up. I will say this once. You have to give me ten lakhs in cash before I pass this. I will ensure that you get 75 lakhs, which means that you will get a net claim amount of 65 lakhs. If I were you, I would take this offer. If you try to report this to anyone, I will deny it outright."

"Right."

"Good. You're a smart man. One needs money to survive in this big bad world. These bloody companies don't pay surveyors well enough. Doesn't matter. We make our wealth from willing donors such as you."

Prakash said, "Yes, sir. I understand."

He gave him a wicked smile. "Good that you understand. Do you want a coffee?"

"No. I'll take off, sir. Thank you for your hospitality."

Prakash walked off from the insurance office. On the door of the office there was a poster which said: *Shah Insurance Consultants and Surveyors – We believe honesty and integrity are the foundations of success.*"

Prakash smiled and thought to himself, "Why am I the one who's stuck with so many self-proclaimed 'honest' people?"

At all levels of public and private offices, the petty functionaries were corrupt to the core. There was no other way to deal with them but to entertain their wishes.

Prakash went back to Chand and presented the offer to him.

Chand immediately said, "We can pay the sum. The issue is how can we be sure he won't back out from the arrangement after we pay him."

"We have to trust him."

Chand said, "Okay. Let's pay him the money and get this over with."

"Right. I'll go back to him in a couple of days and wrap this up."

Prakash went to Dharam the next day.

Jha came up to him and said, "Uday has been acting up again. He came here and threatened to strike if the machines are not restarted and their earlier demands are not met."

Prakash smiled. "Let them strike. Let's take them on this time. I won't pay them salaries for the days that they are not working. What about the other division?"

"They're functioning."

"What are Uday's demands?"

"He wants the machines to be restarted again so that he will once again have the status of a skilled worker. Further, he wants the wages and privileges to be restored as before."

"Right. Tell them we won't do it."

"They'll probably strike and sit outside the factory."

"That is okay. Let them. If we meet their demands, the company will anyway be in a loss. Let us keep the twisting unit shut and the fabric division and texturizing open."

"The fire has helped us in a way. The fabric division workers are firmly against that group now."

"I know. The politicos are a play he will use again but this time we have quite a bit going for us. I don't understand why he isn't ready to leave."

"He is quite affixed on getting you down. He thought you were finished with the death and the fire, but you're back. Now he wants you to fulfil the demands which we had not done earlier."

"Correct. Jha, how did the fire affect the machines?"

"If the coils are burnt, they crash."

"Then our motors have burnt down and the machines are now useless. The insurance money was used for the fabric machines and hence the investment we can make in the yarn division is limited. The repair costs are very high."

"Oh okay. So you're going to plea that the machines are all shut down."

"Right. Let them go to a politico. We will prepare a legit defence this time."

As expected, Uday and Co. approached a labour court again. Jha was summoned to the labour court.

The judge in charge had changed. The new judge was a Mr. Vijay.

As soon as Jha walked into his office, he noticed the workers standing there. Jha started wailing, "Sir, we are ruined. We are finished. Our factory burnt down. The machines which these men were working on are fully finished."

Uday said, "He's lying."

"You can check, sir."

Vijay asked, "Had the company caught fire?"

"Sir, it was the biggest fire to date in this village. We were finished."

He then turned to Uday. "Well, then the machines could have been damaged."

"No, sir the machines are working, he's lying. This man is a liar."

Jha looked at him and started crying again, "Sir, my owner is ruined. He's running whatever machines he could restart. Why will anyone shut down his machines?"

"So, what does he want to do now? Will he let go of these workers?"

Jha asked him in a toned down voice, "Is that possible?"

Vijay shouted, "No. What will happen to these workers? You can't fire them all."

"Okay. But how do we pay them salaries?"

"Tell your owner to give them some other jobs in the factory."

"Can he give them any jobs he wants?"

"Yes."

Uday stared at Jha. This meant Prakash could place them anywhere he liked in the company. Prakash would make them work as helpers. This was completely against his wishes.

Uday protested. "No, sir."

Vijay now raised his voice. "The company has been burnt down. You have to adjust or you can get lost."

He then told Jha, "You wait."

Jha waited behind.

Vijay then asked Jha, "You will have to give me some money for sorting this out."

"Sir, my owner is ruined. He's finished. What will you take from him? Everything is over. He has nothing. He is struggling and on the verge of shut down. Let him recover and we will take good care of you."

"Okay, okay. Get lost then. Handle it your way."

"Okay, sir."

This was the first time that Prakash and Jha did not pay a mediator who had been approached by Uday.

Jha walked out. Uday was waiting for him.

Uday said, "You think you are very smart. I will teach you a lesson."

Uday punched Jha on his face. Jha fell to the ground and blacked out for a second.

He recovered and stared at Uday who was seething in anger. Uday was hoping Jha would retaliate so he could make it a street fight. He had twelve people backing him.

Jha stood up and quietly started to leave.

Uday then shouted from behind. "What happened? You don't have any Bihari blood in you. You are a female in a male's body."

Jha walked off from there retaining in his head what Uday had said. He had realized that was not the time to hit back. There were twelve people with Uday who could hurt him.

He came back and Prakash noted his bruised eye. He immediately asked Sanjay to get a first-aid kit.

"We can get them fired for this."

"No, you can't, because there is no proof that Uday did it. The others will testify against it."

"What are you going to do about it then?"

"I will handle it my way. You now have the mandate to place these guys wherever you like."

Sanjay smiled. "Give me half of this gang."

Jha immediately said, "You can't do anything to them. A supervisor can't harm a worker. But other workers can do what they want."

Sanjay smiled.

Jha called Uday and company to work the next day to place them in alternate jobs.

Uday stared at Jha blankly when he was doing the allocation. He anticipated that Jha would take revenge. Jha did not convey any such emotion. He transferred seven of them to Sanjay's team and the remaining to texturizing as helpers. He was careful to transfer Uday to Sanjay's team.

The Indian Labour Laws classify workers in two groups – Skilled and Unskilled. While the twisting group was classified as skilled when it came to their own work, they were unskilled in other operations and Sanjay and Jha were planning to use them as mere loaders who carried and moved things from here to there. They were quite justified.

By doing this, they had achieved a major goal. The most important issue on the agenda against Dharam was based on minimum wages which were quite impossible for Dharam to meet. The minimum wages of unskilled workers however was a tad below the current wage that Dharam was paying. Things had changed legitimately towards Dharam.

Sanjay came up to Jha after splitting the group. "You have been quite silent after the punch."

"I haven't forgotten it. That punch was a sign of his frustration. It made me very angry. Anything I did at that time could have worsened the situation. Prakash lost his wife and was still calm. I just lost some dignity. If he can come back from that loss, then this was a small sacrifice for me."

"So you've forgiven Uday and are not going to hit him back."

Jha turned and smiled. "Jha...Mahashankar Jha. Wait and watch."

Resurgence

The embodied soul is eternal in existence, indestructible and infinite, only the material body is factually perishable; therefore fight O Arjuna (2.18).

—Bhagvad Gita

"That flower is withering away, Sushma. Let's replace it with another one."

She smiled with a calm face "It's not been treated with love yet. We can water it and bring it back, you know."

"Isn't it worth just bringing another one?"

"If something happens to me, will you replace me or try to bring me back."

Prakash hugged Sushma and gently slapped her. "How dare you say this? Nothing will happen to you. If death approaches you, I will offer myself instead."

Sushma smiled. "You can't live without me, can you?"

"No."

"Prakash...Prakash...."

"What?"

Prakash suddenly got out of his daze. He had fallen asleep on his office chair. He got up, with the sounds of the machines all around him.

The wounds were slowly starting to heal. Death and fire had eroded Dharam's existence but the firm was gradually recovering. The machines were working well in the rented location and generating enough money for the reconstruction work. Prakash was careful not to start the twisting machines. They were anyway a loss-making proposition with all the strikes and the lazing-off that the operators there were used to.

Money that came in because of the machines running was now being used to reconstruct Dharam. Earlier, there were some withdrawals by both Chand and Prakash for non-discretionary expenses. Both minimized their withdrawals to ensure that the firm made a full recovery.

Uday was not done with his struggle yet. He kept badmouthing the company and propagating nonsense about the firm. Ramraj, Foudhar and Kranti who had until then blindly followed Uday were starting to have second thoughts.

Ramraj and Foudhar came up to Jha once and said, "Sir, you've made us helpers. People get promoted but we have been demoted."

Jha looked at them. "Whose fault is it?"

Ramraj said, "Ours. But the penalty should not be this high."

"This is nothing. The real penalty is still to come. Why did all of you align with Uday in the first place?"

"He showed us dreams of more salaries, better facilities and an overall better working life. We fell for those promises and decided to go with the flow."

"You basically thought that you may as well wash your hands while the flow is against the firm. You know the pain that Prakash has gone through is so much that I won't forgive any of you. I will not even let him forgive you. This is now a battle to the end. It's either Dharam or you guys. You did not even give Prakash a chance to explain why your demands were difficult to meet and how things could be worked out. You went to look for a third person to sort out these fights. Now, go find that someone. The only door that will remain in the end will be that of Prakash's. Even if he wants to open an avenue for you, I won't let that happen."

"Sir, why blame us for Uday's mistakes? We are with you. We will work very hard from now on and not listen to Uday."

He then stared at them. "You have chosen a side. If you don't believe in something and yet you chose to stand for it, you have an obligation to stick to it if you want to retain your honour."

"Sir, we don't understand what you are saying. If we don't get food to eat, we can't eat honour."

Jha smiled. "Eating food makes one fat and lazy. Maybe Uday wanted to get rid of that problem for you."

"We are just trapped now, sir. What will happen?"

Jha looked at both of them. "Quit and leave for now. I promise you I will get you back, but you have to quit for now. You both don't seem like trouble makers. I think you should exit with honour."

Both of them walked away contemplating on what Jha had just told them. They had very little choice. No politico was willing to interfere now because they didn't believe much was left, as technically Dharam was following the minimum wage rule which was at the crux of their demands.

Sanjay was party to the conversation from a distance.He walked up to Jha and said, "You've started to break them up."

"I think this is the beginning of the end of a long battle."

"As long as Uday is around, the end will not be that brisk."

"That's true. What can one do but wait? It's amazing, you know."

"What?"

"No labour court, tribunal or politico could guarantee that the problem will completely be solved. Every time they approached an arbitrator, we would solve the problem and hope that we're over and done with. They always managed to find another door. In fact, they would sometimes get the same guy who sorted the problem out to listen to them twice."

"You think that's changed."

"I do. The fire has changed things. We couldn't solve the problem so I guess nature did it for us. It was the ultimate judge and changed our circumstances. That time, your team was almost influenced by Uday as well."

"Jha, it is not over yet."

"It isn't over until we get rid of Uday, but at least the tide has turned. Things look positive now."

"Right."

"You know there are times when I think whether it was totally unfair from their side to demand what they are asking for."

He sighed. "You know I've asked myself this many times. Are we wrong in not meeting their demands? Every time you look at the disparity, it feels wrong. Prakash can afford to eat in the most expensive hotel possible while there are days when these guys are completely out of money and need to ask for loans to ensure there's food at home. It's unfair."

"Yet we try to suppress them."

"What choice do we have? The system is not strong enough to implement these rules for every firm so companies continue to ignore them. If you as a firm implement all the laws as per the book, you are uncompetitive and out of the race. This firm is a provider to many houses and among the rare few that are actually lenient to the workers and their needs. I've never had a better boss than Prakash. Before I joined here, I have worked in four companies. Most bosses are tyrannical. Prakash is gentle as compared to them. The workers here took advantage of that and went completely against him. We either save the interests of more than two hundred workers or we bow down to these thirteen."

"That makes sense."

"Yeah. Sometimes, you have to sacrifice something for the greater good. Isn't that what Lord Krishna told Arjun in the Gita."

"What have you sacrificed?"

"You're asking the wrong question. I have sacrificed absolutely nothing. The right question, my dear Sanjay, is what has Prakash not sacrificed for this firm? He doesn't need to be here but still is to make sure this institution is running. Uday did not commit a mistake by asking for what he was entitled to. He erred by not even giving Prakash a chance to sort things out. When a husband and wife end up taking advice from outsiders, the marriage is bound to end up in a divorce."

"True."

Jha then looked at him and winked. "That's why I keep telling you to not take our fights to our parents."

Sanjay looked at him and playfully said, "Who do I take my worries to, my love?"

Jha seized the moment, "See, I told you one day you will realize that you are the wife in this relationship." He then stroked his moustache yet again. "Jha…Mahashankar Jha."

Uday Shankar Chaubey was at his wits' end. He had started to run out of options. By bringing the salary of the workers down to that of unskilled labourers, Prakash was now incentivizing them to resign rather than throwing them out himself.

Ramraj, Foudhar and Kranti approached Jha behind Uday's back and offered their resignations. Jha immediately cleared their dues and sent them packing with an assurance of giving them a job after he got rid of Uday.

Uday was in Sanjay's unit when he got the news. He had a wrench in his hand and was helping one of the weavers get a machine started. When he found out about what had happened, he was furious. He clenched his teeth and shouted in frustration. He hurled the wrench across the unit and it bounced a couple of times on the floor before it skidded towards one of the walls making a sound that silenced everyone around it.

Sanjay watched Uday vent his frustration but did not make a move. He knew this battle was tilting their way and he did not want to do anything that would harm their position. After about five minutes,

Sanjay indicated to a weaver to hold him and take him out of the firm.

Four or five weavers then held Uday and took him out of the place. He was spewing and spitting around. He was thrown out and Sanjay immediately called for the cleaner to sanitize the place.

Prakash managed to get the insurance amount. He had to do things which were against his conscience but he had realized that if he wanted to see the money he deserved to get, he had no choice. The insurance amount gave Dharam a much needed cushion to operate on.

After work that day, Uday called for a meeting of the remaining activists at his place to plot the remaining course of action. They assembled outside his house. His wife watched silently from the window of the house as the workers assembled in a circle around Uday.

One of them, Mohan, got up and raised the question in everybody's minds, "Is it over for us? Should we search for a job somewhere else?"

Uday paused for a while and replied, "I have one last move. Let me roll the dice one last time before we decide on anything. You have to be with me for one last time."

The other workers looked at each other. They were in doubt and out of steam. A couple of them sighed and said yes.

Uday's fight was not over yet.

Satyagraha

Persons of demoniac nature cannot understand actions that are in their best spiritual interests and actions in their worst spiritual interests; there is never purity nor good conduct nor any truth in them (16.70).

—Bhagvad Gita

Uday and the others knew Prakash could start the machines but was not doing so to prevent them from resuming operation as skilled workers. It irritated them that the other workers were happy. They had been struggling for six months since Dharam had resumed operations and nothing had happened. Time was passing by, their status was getting cemented and Dharam was increasing in stature and power.

Finally, Uday and the nine others who were left behind decided to go on a strike. They sat outside the firm with a banner and went on a strike openly, inviting any other worker who wanted to join them. It was a hunger strike. The wives and kids, though not part of the hunger strike, also joined the workers outside RR.

Their list of demands included restarting the damaged machines and the previous perks/entitlements that they got. It was summer time and the heat was scorching. The heat however didn't matter since it was a battle to the finish for Uday and the others.

They had kept a thin cloth on which nine workers sat in three lines. Uday sat in front of them. They were all profusely sweating but they were in no mood to relent. Uday had decided that he would make Prakash bow down to him, come what may. He also knew this was the best way to get the mediators back in action.

The wives and kids were seated behind the workers. Kids were crying in the heat, yet they were made to sit there to make the situation seem worse to a third party observer and to Prakash.

Prakash hadn't come to office yet nor had he received news of the strike. He had kept a mobile phone with him. Mobiles were relatively new those days, but Jha and Sanjay had decided not to bother him.

Sanjay and Jha walked out to see the state of affairs.

Sanjay looked at Jha. "So it's down to this. The whole village will now know about our problems."

"It's a hunger strike. The dangerous part is that politicos will be happy this has happened. I kind of anticipated this would be their last resort."

"What do you think will happen from here?"

"Make or break. This is the last mile now. Either we admit defeat or they do. We have to ensure no one dies in this strike. If that happens, we are in serious trouble."

"What does that banner say?"

"It says 'Satyagraha – Hunger Strike'."

"How can they demean the word 'satyagraha'? They don't even understand that word. This is more a battle of ego and greed now than a battle for the truth."

Prakash reached office and was staring at what was going on. He just stood there for a while. He had not anticipated this. His strategies were working fine up until then. He was not very perturbed but this was a twist to the tale and one which he had no immediate answer to."

He went in and looked at Jha. "Satyagraha! I feel as if I am an oppressive British ruler."

Jha smiled. "General, what do you think we should do now?"

"I have no idea. I in fact wanted to inform you guys that we should be able to shift back to Dharam in about a month. Clearly, Mr. Uday wants us to shift to hell."

"How many times have you talked to Uday?"

"Not many. In fact, probably the last time was when you had called him down that day."

"Do you want to talk to him today?"

"Okay."

Outside, Uday and the rest of them were silently waiting for someone to come and talk to them.

Prakash went and stood in front of the workers. "Uday, can we talk?"

Uday said, "You say what you want right here. We are all one against your tyranny."

"What tyranny have I done?"

"You have stolen our dignity from us and made us helpers from operators. You are responsible for our suffering and will pay for it."

"Okay. Is there no way we can come at a settlement?"

"Start the machines and make us operators again."

"You will then talk about minimum wages, long paid leaves, tea, coffee and lunches."

"We deserve all of that."

"We can't survive. That twisting operation is the godforsaken one where the margins are so low, we will end up in huge cash losses if I follow all the rules. No competitor is doing that."

"We want you to agree on everything. The law says that you are supposed to give us all that we are entitled for."

"If I do that, you will find something else to strike for."

Uday held Prakash by the hand and took him to his wife. "This is my wife and child. They deserve happiness too. You've taken that away from us."

His wife had kept her head down and his son was crying.

He then shouted on Prakash, "You lost your wife because you're making our families suffer. You rich idiots want to keep all the money for yourself. You don't want anyone to be a part of it."

Prakash went silent when he heard this. He had rudely been reminded of his loss. Jha heard this and rushed out. Sanjay was behind him. Jha looked at Uday in anger and punched him hard on his face. Uday fell down.

Jha stared at him in anger and said, "You dare to say something about Sushma madam. This man does not need to keep this firm running. Yet he is doing that. The companies around you will not even give you the wages and the facilities that Prakash has given you. You talk about your facilities. What about the other workers? Have you ever asked them if they care? Have you not seen how other companies operate? Our houses run because of Prakash's effort. He has nothing to gain from running this firm. How dare you talk about his wife that way?"

Uday was stunned. He had just been thrown to the ground. The other workers did not move.

Jha continued to shout, "If you had any regard for your wife, you would have let Dharam run the way it was. You, however, did not let that happen. There are more than two hundred workers in this firm. Call them out and ask them about Prakash. You are a thankless, frustrated individual who has only hatred to offer."

He then turned to Prakash. "You don't deserve this. You go home. We will handle these hard headed idiots."

Prakash walked into the firm. The mere mention of Sushma had brought tears to his eyes.

Jha walked in after a while.

He looked at Jha. "I loved her so much."

Jha replied, "I know." He paused for a while and then calmly said, "You should go home."

Prakash calmed himself down and looked at Jha. "No."

Sanjay then looked at Jha. "A punch for a punch. You're even with him."

Jha retorted, "This was not for that one. I had forgotten about that. This was because he deserved it for the crappy words he used."

Sanjay sighed. "What godforsaken moment prompted you to recruit this man?"

"Don't ask me that. I've asked myself that a million times and have not got any answer."

Outside, the popular politico, Mr. Yadav had come to express his support for the striking workers. He was as evil as politicos could get. Often, we assume politicos to be a stereotype. We think of them as evil-minded, conniving individuals who only care for themselves. We hope against hope that when we encounter one, he will be different. But, they are quite consistent in who they are and deserve to be admired for their consistency.

Yadav was waiting for an opportunity to get Dharam in the radar again.

Uday walked up to Yadav and said, "We want justice, sir. We will die of hunger unless he meets all our demands."

Mr. Yadav patted him on the back and said, "Son, people like you are heroes because they ensure that the workers get what they deserve."

Jha, Sanjay and Prakash were at the door listening to the conversation. They knew Yadav was probably thanking Uday in his heart that he had given him an opportunity to feed off Dharam again.

Yadav came to Dharam's door and Prakash was expressionless.

"Mr. Prakash, we will make sure that these workers get what they deserve."

Prakash stared at him blankly. Yadav was probably expecting an answer. Prakash was in no mood to give him any answer. He was tired of all the manoeuvring and the evil machinations.

Yadav continued, "Dharam has done everything wrong for these workers."

Prakash collected his thoughts and shot back, "Sir, which Dharam are you talking about?"

"Your company, Dharam. You idiot. Have you forgotten your own firm?"

"Sir, Dharam does not exist anymore. It has burnt down."

"What? It is running right in front of my eyes."

"What you are seeing running is not Dharam, sir. It is RR Enterprises."

"What is there in a name?"

"A lot actually. Technically, this has been running on a different premises and I had to take a license of activities to be run at this premise from your office. We have not taken a licence for twisting because the machines do not work. We might sell them off as scrap soon."

"You have not taken it deliberately so that these men do not get their jobs back."

"I gave them the jobs that I had. The machines don't work. You're welcome to check them."

Yadav looked at him and then said, "I can be on your side, you know."

Prakash looked at him with utter disgust. "Sir, I have been doing some research about you. There are five cases against you that are running. There are a couple of issues I can file a Public Interest Litigation on. It's not that I don't want to pay you. I am tired of this. Stay away from this firm and I will stay away from you.I have nothing to lose now and can go to any extent to save that firm even if it means going against you."

Yadav then turned to Jha, "Your owner has lost his mind."

Jha stared at him with utter disgust. "It feels as if he's just got both his mind and his strength. You can test him."

Yadav decided to walk away from there. Uday tried to stop him but Yadav raised his hand in disgust and walked away.

Uday was shocked at Yadav's reaction. He angrily looked in Prakash's direction and then silently sat down.

Prakash turned to Jha, "How do you break a hunger strike?"

"I don't have any idea. A hunger strike is best broken with food."

"What?"

"If they have food, they will stop."

Prakash looked at him with disgust. "You're joking."

"Sir, we have been through so much, one can't help but sneak a lighter moment here and there."

"Seriously, how do you stop a hunger strike?"

"I have no clue. Uday will only concede if we meet their demands. If any of them get sick, we are in a soup."

Prakash sighed and walked away from there.

Sanjay then came up to him with a glass of water. "Here, have this. Let this go on. You have to maintain that the machines have been damaged because of the fire. You also need to carry on business as usual as far as weaving and texturizing are concerned so that you don't face losses."

Prakash ignored the strike, went to his office and started to work on other issues. He was taking care of the work in other departments when Jha knocked on his door.

Prakash looked up and said, "Come in."

Jha came in. "What do you think we should do?"

"For the short term, I have no idea. For the long term, we have to approach an industrial tribunal and ask them to resolve the issue."

"Will an industrial tribunal rule in our favour?"

"You've got to ensure the machines don't work. We have to obtain an inspection certificate from a qualified engineer that repair will be costly and will take time. If we can prove that it is financially difficult and a time-consuming process to get these machines started, we can state a case saying we only have unskilled jobs for them."

"We can't get all that done immediately, you know. That process will take time"

"No, we can't. But, we have to submit the case to an industrial tribunal to obtain an injunction to prevent such strikes from happening in the future."

"What do we do about this one?"

"We can do nothing but wait to see if we get an opportunity to break it. Their demands are unreasonable and unjust. Uday does not want to negotiate or give an opportunity to the other side at all. I want to get rid of these people."

"You think you will be able to do that?"

"This is my best chance. Dharam had caught fire and the machines were damaged. We can show intent to exit twisting if we are able to show the damaged machines as non-workable."

"Right."

"You have to ensure in your way that the machines look fully damaged because of the fire even to a trained eye."

"Okay."

He then sighed. "I want to get this over with, get this factory running and then hand it over to someone who can give it a reasonable future."

"You want to leave us?" He hugged Prakash in a moment flooded with emotions, "You're not leaving me."

"No, no. But you have to understand, Jha. I have no one left to work for or to take care of the institution. I know rebuilding it was my duty. I owed it to Chand, you people and my wife. Once it is up and running, I can choose to exit it peacefully."

"We can't run this without you."

"You can and I will make sure I hand it over to someone who can run it better than me."

Jha had a tear in his eyes. "We won't stay without you."

"We will see. Anyway, we need to get rid of this menace first.I am open to using any tactics to sort this out, ethical or unethical."

Jha winked, "You are not above employing unethical tactics, are you?"

He then said, "There is nothing ethical about this strike. The word satyagraha means '*the force of truth*'. It is a word conceived by Mahatma Gandhi who said that this force be used to achieve a just end. He advocated giving the opponent an opportunity to talk and achieve a just end. This satyagraha is a farce and against all moral principles. This is a tainted movement based on the tantrums of one man who is somehow of the opinion that we have wronged him and he wants to avenge us regardless of the consequences."

"I regret the day I recruited that man."

"Well, dealing with him was part of Dharam's journey. I think the fire was meant to happen to give us an opportunity to resolve this. No politico or court was ever going to solve Uday Shankar Chaubey for us."

"Let's do this for Dharam. Somehow, I don't get the essence of the firm we worked for in this company."

"Oh yes. This is not Dharam. It is RR. Let's eliminate this menace before we enter Dharam."

Jha sighed. "I hope and pray we are able to end this strike."

Prakash continued his work and Jha left the room.

Sanjay met him outside. "What did he say?"

"He said he is open to using any means necessary to break this strike."

"Do you have any idea on how to break it?"

"None. I don't know but at least we know we can go to any extent we want."

"That's hardly any help if you do not know what you want to do and the extent you want to go to."

Meanwhile, the first day of the strike was coming to an end. They had bought mattresses to sleep outside the factory. They, however, sent their wives and children home for the night and camped outside. It was a full-moon night and the stars were quite clear. The wind was a bit chilly but comfortable. The mood in the camp was sombre.

Jawahar Lal started talking out loud in a frustrated voice, "Looks like we will die here."

Manoj added with a sad voice, "Yes. Uday, are you sure this is worth all that we are going through?"

Uday looked at them red-faced. "They have given us helper level jobs. They will pay for it."

Jawahar continued, "We have followed you blindly up until now. We haven't got increased salaries."

Uday wanted to shout at Jawahar but kept his cool. "We had won earlier. Have you forgotten that? You are all part of a team and a bigger goal. We cannot quit now. It is a matter of a few days. He will have to sort it out. If something happens to any of you, he will be in deep trouble."

"You mean that something has to happen to one of us for this to end?"

Uday gave Jawahar a frustrated look. Jawahar noted that Uday was getting angry so he kept quiet. He realized that anything could set off a fight between him and Uday and it was prudent for him to keep his cool.

The rebels were, however, feeling lost. Before the fire, they had got a lot of support from the politicos, union leaders and had gotten one or the other of their demands met. They had hardly worked since Uday had given them direction and were answerable to no one. It all seemed rosy then and Uday was a demi-god for them.

The tide had turned after Dharam caught fire. They were suddenly reduced to helpers, their salaries slashed and work profiles were radically changed on the behest that the machines they worked on were damaged and hence non-workable. Earlier when they made a ruckus, one or the other door answered but this strike did not find any traction. Yadav had walked away and seemed to have disowned them. Uday was planning to take this satyagraha to an industrial tribunal or court but they were not so confident this time that a court would entertain them.

Before Jha left for home on day one of the satyagraha, he came face to face with Uday.

Jha looked at him with disgust and asked him, "What the hell do you think you are doing?"

Uday shot back, "This is satyagraha. A man like you will not understand."

Jha smiled. "This is not satyagraha. Satyagraha is the force of the truth. What you are doing is throwing tantrums. This is not a struggle. It is a desperate man trying hard to hang on to a thin thread before it breaks."

He then started to move away. Before he left, he turned to Uday. "An ethical man knows when he is right or wrong. You have lost track of that boundary. Today, not only Prakash but the entire workforce of Dharam is against you. Do not damage the meaning of the word satyagraha coined by the Mahatma. Back off now and let's work this out."

Uday's eyes were red. "This may not be satyagraha for you, but it is one for us. It is now a fight to the end."

Jha kept his hand on Uday's shoulder and said, "The end is very near, my friend."

Uday brushed it away. "Very near, indeed."

Jha smiled, clenched his teeth and ran his fingers over his moustache. "Jha…Mahashankar Jha."

Almost instinctively, Uday responded back twirling his moustache. "Chaubey…Uday Shankar Chaubey."

Jha was stunned. Uday had just fleeced his style. He couldn't help but smile and walked away from the scene.

Dharamyudh – The Fight for Duty

You cannot not choose sides in a battle for duty. You are either on the side of the truth or the side of the wrong.

—Bhagvad Gita

The sunset was beautiful. The light was serene was, as if the sun was becoming one with the ocean. The sky was painted in gold and the overall effect was very calming.

Sushma kept her head on Prakash's shoulders and said, "We should take snaps so that we can relive these memories."

"I have formed images of these in my head."

She then pretended to be slightly upset and folded her arms akin to an indignant child, "That is just because you don't want to buy a camera."

"No, I don't take photographs because then you'll show it to people and their jealousy would have an ominous effect on our relationship. I have all my memories imprinted right here in my head."

"Don't worry. I'm not going to leave you until I die."

Prakash woke up. He stared at the empty room he was in. He got up and got himself a glass of water.

He then walked out of the room to give himself some air. There was no one at home. His mother had gone to visit his sister for a few days and he was all alone. He was not able to sleep because he was getting recurring dreams about Sushma.

Meanwhile, things at Dharam were pretty much status quo with the workers still waging their war. The dharna was pretty much on and in full swing.

A well-built worker from Sanjay's group, Mohan Biswas, was on his way to work. He suddenly stopped midway and looked at Jawahar. "Did you say something about me?"

Jawahar was slightly taken aback, "No, I did not."

Mohan's eyes grew red. "You said something about me being an idiot."

Jawahar was blank. The other workers were quite weak and tired because they had had no food for many days and were not quite alert so they had not noticed anything.

Uday then intervened and approached Mohan. "He did not say anything. Now please go."

Meanwhile, a few other workers from Sanjay's group who were also close 'aides' of Mohan stood behind him.

Uday realized that they were there to fight. So, he held back and started to walk away from them.

Mohan held him and said, "Who are you to tell me to go? You are the outsider here, not me." He then roughly pushed Uday towards the other workers.

Uday never had the capacity to control his temper. He was an impulsive man who reacted at the slightest provocation. He knew in his head this was planned. Yet, he couldn't hold back and punched Mohan on his face. The other workers from Sanjay's group were waiting for this and they pounced on the other rebels who were sitting outside.

This was a streetfight. Jha had already called the police. Within five minutes of the brawl, the police interrupted. They separated the brawling workers and arrested all of them. They were all taken to the local police station. Prakash was not present at the factory at that time as per plan so that he could claim complete ignorance about what had happened.

While the police was escorting the workers out of the area, Uday stared at Jha who was talking to the police officer at that time. He realized he had been had. Jha looked at him and gave him a pleasant smile.

The workers were booked on several grounds of assault, battery and public nuisance. These offences under the Indian Penal Code provided for a penalty or punishment or both. They were, however, bailable offences.

Jha went to the police station with the rebels and the police. He went with them as a witness to give a first-hand account of the situation. He did not file an FIR and left that to the police who did the same suo moto. Jha gave his testimony after which he quietly walked away from there and went back to the factory where Sanjay was waiting for him.

Sanjay immediately looked at him, "Should we call Prakash?"

"No."

"So. Has your plan worked?"

"We don't know yet."

"Even my men are in jail."

"Not for long. If I bail them out now, it will be evident that we caused this. Let's hang on for a while."

"I need to inform their families and pay them their daily wage."

"You know a few wives would be happy that their husbands are in jail and the income is coming straight to them instead of coming after it has been washed away or depleted by a bottle of alcohol."

"Yeah. Your wife would pay the company good money to keep you in jail, Jha."

"Very funny. Let's inform Prakash that our plan is on track as of now."

"Why did you make sure that he wasn't here when this happened?"

"It's easier for him when he answers to anyone who asks him about this. Everything happened behind his back so it becomes difficult to implicate him."

"You're a cunning man. Some would even call you evil."

"This was not my plan."

"Prakash thought of all this?"

"Every little bit. There is a devil behind the god we know."

Sanjay smiled.

Back in the jail cell, the workers were stunned at what had happened. They were all stacked in a single cell and weren't fighting anymore. They were now staring at possible imprisonment and were shell-shocked. Sanjay's employees weren't that worried because they knew it was part of a plan.

There was silence and an atmosphere of fear all around. Jawahar was the first one to break down and he wailed to the officer in charge, "Sir, we did not do anything. Please get us out of here. We don't deserve to be here. We were only asking for our rights."

Manoj walked up to him to calm him down a bit.

He kept his hand around Jawahar's shoulder and told him, "Everything will be all right. All this is very temporary."

The cell was a small one – about 10x10 with a small toilet in the corner. It was a hell hole. Twenty workers were all stacked inside two such cells. It was extremely claustrophobic and the atmosphere was quite morbid.

Om Prakash Yadav walked up to Uday. "Do you have a solution for all this?"

Uday stared at him with blank eyes. He did not have the money for bail and had not anticipated this situation at all. He was lost for words. No politico was ever going to help them get bail because that meant spending money and politicians were used to resolving disputes where they got money and not where they had to spend it.

Back in the factory, Prakash was still missing. Jha and Sanjay were deliberating their next move. The factory was functioning normally without disruption. There were murmurs inside the company with people talking about what had happened with the striking workers. There were rumours that it was all part of the company's plan.

Jha and Sanjay were mum on the issue. A few workers approached them to find out if the workers were behind bars because of them.

When asked if he was involved, Jha responded with indignance, "If I wanted to repair their minds, I could have done it single-handedly. I did not need help for that. They fought among themselves. This is what happens when there is no respect for the company. They did not have any respect for each other as well. Now, they are all in jail and God knows how long they will stay there."

When Jha was alone, Sanjay came up to Jha and said, "You think we were wrong to have done this?"

"There is no wrong and right. This was for Dharam, hence it was a *Dharamyudh* (fight for duty). We fought for what we thought was right. They are fighting for what they think is right. We lost the battle before and were in a risk of losing the entire firm. All the workers were starting to think like Uday. In a way, Dharam's biggest disaster, the fire, was our biggest blessing and the only chance we had of eliminating them. Think of the number of workers who would be out of jobs. It was virtually impossible for Prakash to compete in the market if all of Uday's conditions were satisfied."

"Wasn't our move a desperate one by someone who has run out of options?"

"Desperate times call for desperate measures. So what? We were up against the wall. What did Uday expect Prakash to do? Prakash tried to convince him to talk and discuss the issues. The company would not have survived if he agreed to everything. Other owners in the industry are far more unfair."

"Well…"

Jha continued, "He knew that, yet he wanted to talk and sort it out. Uday played whatever card he could and assumed Prakash was wrong right from the start. He used politicians, courts and all means available to him. There was no room for any negotiation. Prakash was the villain and that was it."

"Yet, the conclusion seems very harsh."

"It is what it is. If things don't happen the linear way, you twist your fingers to get work done. I don't regret any move we have made."

Uday was quietly seated in a corner of the jail cell. He was staring at the ceiling. Life had been unfair right from the start and had continued to be so with him. He had almost gotten Prakash to his knees had it not been for the fire. Prakash for him was an oppressor just like his father. He had cornered Prakash but things had turned drastically and gone out of his control. He never in his wildest dreams imagined that he would end up in a cell with the other workers.

His head was throbbing and his body was in pain, He sat down on the floor leaning against the walls of the jail cell and closed his eyes for a while.

"Maa, have you had your food? Why are you crying?"

She cleaned her eyes quickly and looked up at Uday. "Nothing, son. I was just remembering your father."

"Don't cry, Maa. Things will become okay. We have nothing to do with that man now. I hit him real hard."

She stared at him. "You were very angry with him. Don't ever get so angry with anyone again. Not everything is resolved by a fight."

"This world is unfair, Maa. You have to fight to get what you want. No one helps you out."

She hugged him. "No beta. That is not true. Life may be unfair to us in some aspects but it will be fair to us in others. God gave me a bad husband but also gave me a very good son."

Uday looked at her with tears in his eyes. "No, Maa. The rich have it all while we have nothing. I have no money, no education and no father. Life is unfair."

"Things will become okay one day."

A worker woke Uday up. "Uday, get up. Jha is here."

Jha stared at Uday. "I have a proposal."

Uday was silent.

"I will bail you out but all ten of you have to resign and forget about Dharam. You have to forget you were ever here. We will clear your dues on a fair basis."

Uday looked at the other nine workers but did not respond. He was dejected and lost.

Jha immediately said, "You can think about it. I will also convince the officer to remove all charges against you."

He walked away from there to give the workers time to think. After he left, the workers started to gather up. Meanwhile, Jha bailed Mohan and his workers out and ensured no formal charges were placed against them. He left the ten workers behind and left.

Jawahar started the conversation, "Will we really lose our jobs?"

Uday replied, "I don't know but it looks as if that will happen now."

Omprakash Yadav hit his hand on his head and shouted, "Where will we go? I have heard the other companies have bosses much worse than Prakash sir. You do not get wages on time, bonuses or leave wages." He then looked at Uday in anger, "You have caused all this. Prakash Sir was not that unfair. You corrupted our minds."

Uday looked at him and said, "All this while when we were winning and people were with us, you thought he was unfair. You wanted to get the benefit of higher wages and perks. Now when we are losing, you think he was fair?"

"Yes. You've bought us to a situation where we have nowhere to go. We should ask Prakash sir for forgiveness and to take us back."

Uday replied, "We should not ask for forgiveness."

Omprakash Yadav looked angrily at him. "You better shut up. We have had it with you. People like you mess with our heads and take us in the wrong direction."

Uday was silent till then, but couldn't take it anymore. He held Omprakash Yadav by the collar. "You are a chameleon who changes sides whenever he wants. You are right. I was fighting for the wrong people."

The other workers separated the two of them. There were a few abuses exchanged after which Umesh Yadav spoke up. "Enough. We will ask Prakash sir for forgiveness. Uday, it is not about changing sides. It is about knowing when to accept defeat. We have to realize that we were wrong in our ways as well. There has to be an end to this."

Uday looked at him. The battle was over and the white flag had just been drawn. The final round belonged to Prakash, Jha, Sanjay and Dharam.

Uday had given up. He had made up his mind to resign. He was sure of one thing, though. He was not going to apologize or ask for forgiveness.

Elimination

From anger comes delusion; from delusion, confused memory; from confused memory the ruin of reason; from ruin of reason, man finally perishes (2.63).

—Bhagvad Gita

Prakash looked at his dad. "Why do you work so hard, Dad? We have enough money now. I am well settled in my job and Nima will get married off soon. You should relax now."

Manohar smiled "After a point, Prakash, it is not about the money. It is a dream that you build for your kids and for all the people associated with the firm. Dharam is more than just a place of work now. It has become a part of our existence. Part of our souls, even after we pass away, will be part of Dharam."

"Dad, you are not going to leave me. Don't say such things. You think I'll be capable enough to take over the firm. Are you just doing all this to give me a legacy?"

"Dharam is an idea, son. We want a firm in the textile industry which will be good to its employees and yet remain profitable. I hope you will carry the idea forward. If not you, we hope we find somebody else who will."

"I do not see myself being capable of indulging with labour, Dad. I don't know if I can ever do that. I've heard there are labour problems, union conflicts and many other problems of this sort. It's just too scary."

"Life teaches you, Prakash. Life and experience are the best teachers. If it is destined, you will learn to face these problems head on."

Prakash took his eyes away from his father's picture hanging on the wall of his cabin and couldn't help but wonder whether Manohar would have handled this situation better than he had. He sighed and walked outside where there was a line of workers waiting for him. All of them had just come out of jail and were shaken up. They were scared that they would lose their jobs. Jha had informed the police officer in front of them that if these workers did not comply with what they had promised, he would like him to press charges and give him back the security money. All of them had come with their wives and children so that there would be some sympathy towards them.

Simultaneously, Dharam was almost ready. None of these ten were ever going to work in the rejuvenated firm that now looked better and stronger.

Prakash came in to deliver the final settlements that day. It was a sunny day and the children were crying out of thirst.

He saw the workers and looked at Jha. "What are they waiting for?"

"For their final settlements. They've all agreed to resign together."

"Jha, first give these women and children some water and food. We'll talk to these workers after that."

He then looked at the workers. "Please send them home. If anything, their presence will make things worse."

Jha got some food and drinks for the women and children and started to send them home. One among them refused to go home and was silent but in tears. She was Uday's wife, Savitri, and had decided that she would be with her husband right to the end.

Uday looked at her and his son and told them to go. They refused to budge.

Prakash looked at her and Uday's son. He then walked up to Uday's wife. "I assure you I will not let his interests be spoiled by whatever happens today. Let me talk to him."

She looked at him with tears in his eyes, "Sir, please let me be with him. Life has been unfair with my husband and so has his luck. If I stand by his side, I can correct him if he goes wrong."

Prakash took a deep breath and said, "Okay." He then turned to Jha. "Jha, get her and the child a chair. Ensure that they are given water and food."

Jha nodded.

Sanjay then came up to him. "Sir, there is a task to be done today before we move to Dharam tomorrow."

"What?"

"We have to let go of these workers today so that Dharam can start afresh. We have to erase the past before we move into the new facility."

All the workers except Uday heard this and shouted, "No, no. Please don't throw us out."

They then looked at Uday, "He misled us."

Uday was very silent that day. He was remorseful to a degree, yet a part of him said that he had been right in demanding what the law had set out for him. He knew, however, that he was all alone and all out of everything he had.

Prakash said, "Let's talk inside."

The workers started to move inside. Prakash sat down in his office and the workers formed a group around the table. Notably, Uday did not come in. He stayed outside with Savitri and his child.

"Sir, please forgive us. We have nowhere to go. We were misled by that man outside."

Prakash smiled. "You have turned on him. You were with him when it was in your interest to do so. He may be wrong but at least he took a stand and stuck with it. That man could not be bought, negotiated with or bartered with. I think he did everything for you. I, on the other hand, did everything I could to save others. Both were probably never on the wrong side. You guys are turning on him which makes you untrustworthy. You were with him when it served your interest and went against him when the tide turned against you."

The workers gave Prakash a surprised look. "You are defending him."

"No, but his fight was with me, not with you. If you did not want to take part with him, you should have elected to do so earlier. Now is not a time to choose. I can't retain any of you. I can't take the risk of you turning against Dharam again. You guys have a history of turning against those who fight for you."

"Sir, Uday was the one who is to be blamed for all this."

"Right, but you are no saints either. You are not kids to be led. You saw it beneficial to join him in struggle then, so you conveniently joined him, now you see him on the losing side, so you are apologizing to me."

"Sir, please forgive us."

He turned to Jha. "Please take their resignation letters formally and give them their entire dues. Make sure you give them Rs. 2000/- extra each so that they get a start from here."

Jha replied, "Okay."

He called each one of them and started working on their settlement amounts. Even though they had joined together, a few of them had taken some loans and some of them had settled earlier and rejoined. So, the settlement amounts were not huge. Prakash made sure that they received the entire settlement as per law, including the gratuity amount if they were entitled to it.

Vijay Kumar, while taking his settlement, fell down on his knees before Jha and touched his feet. "Sir, I don't want to find another job. We will work on your terms. Don't throw us out of Dharam."

Jha blankly stared at him. "I can't do anything here. I've been ordered by the boss to let you guys go."

"He will listen to you."

Jha looked at him with anger in his eyes. "Did you listen to me earlier? You did not even think it worth talking to me. I got hit in front of all of you and no one came ahead to help. I was hit on the face but the injury was affixed to my heart. I love my firm, my boss and I will do anything to keep him out of harm's way. Dharam has to work without you to survive. You are who you are. You will not change. When the opportunity and the right leader comes back, you will strike again."

The others heard this discourse and started to collect their settlements and signed on stamped vouchers. Jha was doing this with a resolve which showed on his face.

Nine people signed the vouchers and took their settlements. They were courteously shown the way out.

There was one man left, the leader of the resistance, Uday. Everyone including Jha was staring at the family standing outside. His signature on that stamped voucher would signal the end of a battle that had lasted for nine years. Except the end, he had fairly been in control the entire time, but looked defeated now.

Uday sighed and looked at his wife. The other workers had left. It was just him now. He kissed Savitri and his son on the forehead and headed towards Jha.

Jha very quickly drew up the final settlement, added the Rs 2000 and was going to get the voucher signed. Prakash stopped him. He called Savitri inside the office.

He looked up at Uday. "What prompted so much hatred?"

Uday smirked. "I thought you were making money from our efforts and we were being wronged."

"Why didn't you give me a chance to explain?"

"You would somehow convince the team and make them go back to work on the same terms as before."

"You have to understand I'm in a market which plays it dirtier than me."

"That doesn't give you a licence to do wrong things."

"No, it does not. If you would have given me a chance to talk, I would have tried to come up with something innovative to keep myself and you alive and in the market. I can't be isolated. You, however, kept my back against the wall all the time. I was forced to go to every tribunal and politico possible."

He then turned towards Savitri, "Do you fight with him?"

"Yeah."

"Do you complain about it to your mother and other relatives?"

"No."

"Why not?"

"Such matters should be kept within the household."

He then looked at Uday. "You hear that. This is not a company. It is a family. Such quarrels should be kept within. When outsiders interfere, they take more than what they give to either side."

Uday sighed. "What do you want?"

"An apology would be good for all I have gone through."

He looked at him and said, "I'm sorry for all I've done."

Prakash turned to Jha. "We owe him arrears for the minimum wage. I don't know what the calculation is but he fought for this knowing it was right. We owe it to him so that he leaves from here knowing it was fair and square. Give him an additional Rs. 5000 so that he gets some time to get back on his feet."

Savitri looked at Prakash. "Thank you, Sir."

"I told you I won't let him be harmed."

Uday blasted out. "I don't want your charity, sir."

Savitri looked at him with anger. "Calm yourself down and accept what you get. You have to control your temper if you ever want to see your son have a good life."

Uday calmed down and Jha summed up his farewell package. He collected it and started to walk out. All three – Jha, Sanjay and Prakash – stared at Uday's back when he was walking out of the firm. It was symbolic for them.

Jha collapsed on his seat. "I have no words. It is finally over."

"Yeah."

Prakash smiled after a very long time. Sanjay got three glasses of water and gave Jha and Prakash one each.

He then rose his glass, "Sir, I have seen this on television. They raise their glasses and say a toast."

Prakash winked at him, "I think that is with alcohol."

Jha said, "This water is as good as alcohol. It is getting me high."

Prakash said, "Cheers then, to Dharam."

Jha and Sanjay simultaneously raised their glasses. "Cheers."

The Journey Beyond

My illusion has been dispelled, O Krishna, by your grace realization is restored to me; I am stable and all my doubts are removed. I shall execute your command (18.73).

—*Bhagvad Gita*

"We started off as a small firm and have covered a lot of distance over the years. A lot of it has been you, the workers and the team here. Many people focus on the management of a firm when it has become successful but in reality, it is a team, a family which takes a firm to its glory. At any point if the management goes wrong or if the workers go wrong, there has got to be a peaceful resolution process. That is essential for the survival of this institution. My father named it Dharam because it was his father's name. I have rebuilt this institution and have the option to rename it, but I prefer we call it Dharam. The word signifies what it means to us. For me, it signifies something that my wife would have loved to see in all its glory. It is a religion, the tenets of which are hard work, trust and honesty. Most importantly, it is a means to bring to life some dreams of all of you, however small or big they may be."

Jha shouted loudly, "Three cheers to Dharam and Prakash."

The crowd shouted back in unison.

There was lunch organized that day for all the workers. It was quite a sumptuous buffet. Few among the workers had opted for the duty of serving others. Wives and kids were invited as well and Prakash had ensured there was enough food for everybody.

There was a celebration fit for kings. The day was significant for the workers. They were moving back to the firm that many a time had seemed on the verge of closure.

Jha walked up to Prakash. "Dharam has come a long way. These walls have seen a lot."

"Yeah."

"What next?"

"Chand isn't keeping very well. We might need another hand so I have asked his son-in-law to join the firm. He's a very nice guy and seems keen. It will be a way of passing his share to him and keeping the firm intact."

"What about you?"

"I'm with you guys for now. I haven't really thought about where I want to go from here. For now, I need to get this firm to run so that there is no interruption in anyone's life. I'm here for the next few years so don't stress about it."

Jha sighed and hugged him. "I'm not leaving you until I die."

Prakash patted his head and said, "Yeah. You're my second wife. After the first one left me, you're my only hope."

"Does it feel like she's around?"

"Yeah. It felt like that when we entered here. It felt as if she was smiling. She looked content."

"You miss her?"

"A lot. It hurts every moment. I try to focus on work so that for a while I don't feel her absence, but she's around."

"Her blessings and presence have kept Dharam alive."

"I think of what Chand said that day all the time when he threw her ashes on the ground here. She is the foundation of Dharam and when the foundation of a firm is of such a pure heart, then how can anything bad ever happen to it?"

Jha smiled. "This firm will become much bigger than it is one day. Mark my words, Prakash."

Prakash walked out for some fresh air. He stood in the compound, looking straight towards the building.

"You know, Prakash, this is a weaving machine. It makes fabric."

"It must be difficult no, Dad. You take care of so many people. It is so easy for anyone of them to get annoyed or angry with you."

"The trick, son, is to be patient and fair with the people working for you."

"The firm is lucky to have you, Dad."

"It won't have me forever, Prakash. You have to take over one day when I am no more."

Prakash was in tears. "You will never leave me, Dad."

Uday meanwhile had applied to another firm for a job as a supervisor and was called for an interview. This firm was primarily into yarn processing.

"So, you were working in Dharam."

"Yes."

"Why did you leave that company? It is a big company and we have heard the owner is a good man."

"The twisting machines burnt down and could not be repaired."

"Okay."

"Are you a good team-player?"

Uday smiled, "Yes. I am good with people. They tend to listen to me."

"Good and you know how to operate these machines well, right?"

"Like the back of my hand."

"Hmm...Are you aggressive? We don't like aggressive and rebellious people."

Uday looked at the manager in his eyes and said, "No, sir. I am quite docile."

Change is
The Law of The Universe

BHAGVAD GITA

Whatever happened, it happened for good;
Whatever is happening is happening for good;
Whatever will happen, it will be for good;
What have you lost for which you cry?
What did you bring with you which you have lost?
What did you produce which was destroyed?
You did not bring anything when you were born;
Whatever you have you have received from Him;
Whatever you will give you will give to Him;
You came empty handed and you will go the same way.
Whatever is yours today was somebody else's yesterday and will be somebody else's tomorrow;
Change is the law of the universe.

Coming Soon - From the Same Author

I WANT TO LIVE

"What is this life if it is not worth dying for something?"

– Martin Luther King.

"While she was in the hospital fighting for her life, she looked at me and asked for a piece of paper and a pen. I thought she wanted to tell me who did this to her so I could fight for her. I thought she wanted to tell me to take revenge and make that guy pay but she didn't write that. On that piece of paper, she wrote something that will haunt me for the rest of my life."

The group stared at me, tears in all of their eyes as well. One or two even held me close and tried to calm me down.

I took out the piece of paper from my pocket and put it down in front of absolute strangers who had but just one thing in common.

The paper said: 'Dhruv, I want to live….'

Bravado and craziness often go together and need a motive. There has to be reason for someone who puts everything on the line. I guess I was holding on to a thought, the essence of being in love with someone. It was a crazy idea, just the feeling of being at that place in your life. When you wander without a purpose, you get the feeling you're drowning and that time's running out. You hold on to that first hand you can see so that you don't sink in.

That hand has to be it. The love of your life, the person you were supposed to spend the rest of your life with and all that jazz. After a while, you don't check back on that feeling. You don't give it a beta test or anything.

Now imagine the aforesaid hand snatched away from you. If that happens, the response of the man who almost drowned could be so extreme that the outcome can potentially surprise you.

I was that man, the individual without direction. I was born with a golden spoon and I had no intention to make it into a diamond one. I wasn't one of those youngsters who had any drive. For me, life was a random process, the outcome of which was so heavily dependent on luck that you might as well enjoy it on the way. My life was full of travels and adventures funded by my late father's interest generating instruments.

I was aptly named Dhruv, living the life fit for a prince. But for all the randomness that life has to offer, one would least expect me to be hit by sticks and face tear gas. When that sacrifice didn't work, I had all but one shot of the gun to offer. My life had come down to getting this right. All I could think of when I was taking it was her. No one except two random men knew that I was doing this and there was a good chance that, win or lose, in both situations, no one would ever bother to find out why I did what I did.

Life had taken me from being the reckless globetrotter to the fundamentalist murderer. They say it can be very weird and change each and every fundamental truth in and around you whenever the hell it desires to. It doesn't take much, a few years, months, days or even moments for you to awaken to a new reality. For the lucky ones, that reality is love. For unfortunate ones like me, the reality was loss.

Maybe, I still am the prince but in a different sense. Perhaps, I was meant to be '*Che*'. These are my motorcycle diaries.